Teller
of Tales

RAY DACOLIAS

Teller of Tales

ISBN 978-0-9888177-2-2

Contents

Janitor

There is a thick wood with many sparkling streams and diverse fauna and foliage and a bouquet of smells that perfume the air with their sweet intoxication. There is no need of Man and his machinations, no need of Man and his aspirations, no need of Man and his aggressive nature to rip and shred and tear and despoil the land; but Man does come, he always comes and he always destroys that which Nature hath delicately wrought; it is Man's fate to seize that which is sublime and humble and violate its inherent richness and innocence with his own indecency and disrespect and rebuild it in his own ugly image. So goes Man, until he goes away forever and leaves Nature to resurrect the land and begin anew—it is true, Man can blow open the hard guts of the earth and pour in his toxic will and pollute the inner core and outer core with his vile wastes, and after Man has finally dissolved back to dust, Nature will find balance and harmony and the land will flourish once again.

But it is the fate of Man to inhabit the earth now. He plants his strong foot into the soil and he builds monuments unto himself; he erects great structures and creates wealth from the difference between what is necessary and what is not, what is good and what is bad, who has too much and who has too little; this Man does, he pursues his own lot as he stretches his muscular arm across the wilderness—and in doing so, divisions arise, divisions of race and creed, divisions of gender and religion, divisions of color and age, divisions of beauty and homeliness, and any individual that Man decides is not worthy of the highest rank and order according to the dictates of his law falls into his own crushed and crowded division.

In any society, then, there exist these divisions—these castes, these rankings—and in every society it is different, based on one precept here, on another there, but in the end, all societies adopt them and sleep with them like a seductive mistress.

How do these divisions happen? It is too much to ponder, now, but it is not too much to study the history of one society that is not unlike any other society in the way it suspends the rights and dignity of some and elevates the status and achievements of others. Let us, then, explore a small section of American society, where it has been decided that people who do not possess a certain racial profile or even a job that necessitates a higher education have earned less respect and dignity than the general public.

There is a public high school. Its location is not important, for what is important is that it is like any other high school, in that it has the same physical structure and societal hierarchy of other high schools. Everyone has a ranking and everyone knows his place in line and everyone knows how to stay within the tight boundaries of that space or he is generally spanked and quickly put back into line. It is a system that has nothing to do with fairness, and more to do with the culture of the place. It simply is, and always will be.

The principal is the chief and the assistant principal is second in command and the teachers and the guidance counselors are next on the status pole, and after them everyone else is planted on the same awkward and narrow rung—the teachers' assistants and the security officers and the cafeteria workers and the maintenance workers—but also on that precious lower rung rest the custodians. Now, at big high schools there are even divisions, albeit small ones, between the players on each level, but at small high schools, the divisions widen even more, which leads us to one school in particular.

This high school was in a small town. The people here are like any other people in any other small town, as they have their own prejudices and predilections for people and things, their own ideas but mostly other people's ideas about the world, and mostly the ideas of dead people or confused people or people they would have scorned had they known them; yet this is the way it is, that people adhere to a thinking pattern based on what came before them and what percolates down to them from the filthy skies and what little education inhabits their virgin brains. But these people were about to receive a small lesson in the danger of judging a human by his skin color and lack of education.

In this town there were precisely one thousand two hundred and thirty-eight people, and of those one thousand two hundred and thirty-eight people, exactly one thousand two hundred and thirty-seven of them had the same outer complexion.

When Sam Washington left his humble farm and came into town, the people generally stared and whispered, and when he walked past people and smiled and tipped his blue and white baseball hat at the womenfolk, the people generally stopped and stared; and when he walked into shops to buy his supplies, people generally stopped talking and stared and shook their collective heads and hemmed and hawed and expelled exasperated breaths and showed countenances of incredulity. The power of this one man to shut down this thriving and healthy Midwestern town was truly remarkable.

"Why do he have to be here, in our little town," the manager of the general store said as he watched Sam get into his old Chevy truck, which was always clean on the outside and immaculate on the inside, and then drive away down the lazy boulevard. "I mean, shoot, we ain't no cosmopolitan city here, he jus' don' blend in none."

"He like a black bean in a sack of white rice," one of his loyal customers replied, without much thought, as he had already established his own idea on the subject long ago.

"An' don' a feller normally pick that there oddball colo' outta that there mess of grains to be sure'n they ain't spoiled?" the manager replied.

"Sure enough," interjected another male customer, who was wearing blue overalls and a straw hat and sucking on a long yellow straw. "Only way to be safe is ta remove the rocks and grit and whatnot from the mix."

The general manager frowned as he looked at the slow-moving truck that was trailing off down the road. "I reckon he don' know that, and I knowd people dun told him that—that he just don' fit in here," and he lifted his flabby arm towards the street as his voice became exasperated, "but you can plainly see he ain't listening."

"No, he ain't a good listener, a'tal."

"Sometimes I do wonder if he is deaf."

"Don't think so, I knowd he hear me when I talk to him 'bout his bill—you know, he always pays on time, and that is something curious, too; most folks likes to stretch it out a bit, but not ol' Sam—it's always cash on the barrelhead with him. Curious."

"Is mighty curious."

"And how long he been a living here, anyway—'bout twenty year?"

"'Bout twenty-five year, came here after the war with his sweetheart but she up and died and now he is as quiet as a church mouse—and no complaints 'bout him, neither, excepting that he is a black bean in a sack of white rice."

"Jus' that, I reckon."

It was the kind of town where everybody knew everyone and everybody knew everyone's business and one could not move left or right from the acceptable center without the entire town commenting on it, to wit: one fine Autumn day, two of the knuckleheaded boys of the town decided to do a truly knuckleheaded thing, and that was to rob the local general store; well, sir, those two teenaged, pimple-faced knuckleheads walked right into the store, each of them wearing a tight brown stocking over their round head and sporting an unloaded handgun and demanding money from the manager, to which he replied, just as if he were speaking to his own children, "Well, Zack and Henry, I reckon that after I call your folks and tell 'em what ya'll been up to, you might just want to actually get some books to put down your skinny britches."

The two kids hightailed out of there just like rabbits that had happened upon a council of coyotes.

This town was a microcosm of society. What any town needed, it had: a doctor, a lawyer, a sheriff, a school, a church, a fire department, merchants and workers, high rollers and low rollers, loafers and worker bees, busybodies and quiet ones—and if all of these roles and titles were put into a bag and shaken up and then poured out onto a table, there would appear a natural order from bottom to top. It is the same everywhere. The handsome boys get the girls and the ugly boys get the sweat. The powerful people do as they please and the ordinary people get the blood and sweat. The rich folk get the favors and the poor folk get the blood, sweat and tears.

It was now the morning of the high school prom, a prestigious event as any could be imagined in this small town. Around these parts there was only the Fourth of July that had a greater scale of excitement, all because Fred Logerson had a fireworks machine and the entire town always congregated at the high school stadium to see the great event. The students talked about the prom for months prior to its occurrence and the adults tried not to think about it at all; but then the realization would come upon them that committees would have to be formed and once again they were, and so preparations began to ensure that the event would be a huge success.

And Sam Washington was right in the middle of it, an integral part not to be discarded, as he was the sole janitor for the high school. He was very good at what he did and he always did his job without complaining or questioning his superiors, and all of this was accomplished despite a few things he encountered daily, to wit:

"Hey, janitor, you missed a piece of paper here," one student would say, sneering.

"Hey, janitor, could you move a little faster, I want to get to class before the sun burns out," a teacher would say.

"Hey, janitor, didn't I tell you to clean up the mess in Room 12?" the principal would say.

And Sam, for that was his name—but you would not have guessed it had you been present at the school—dressed in his blue denim overalls, would merely nod his head to such utterances and proceed to accommodate those around him, never frowning or evincing emotion of any kind; and because of this, he was freely mocked and derided by nearly everyone there—"nearly everyone" is stated here because those closest to him in societal rank were the only ones who called him by his Christian name and spoke to him civilly. He had been a long time at his job and no one ever thought about terminating him, simply because no one else in town wanted it.

Still, it was the night of the prom and there was panic everywhere, just as there is for every grand gathering, and there was Sam preparing the gymnasium with a steady hand and a cool head amongst the uproar and chaos of the students and faculty; and still, they yelled at him and heaped scorn upon his head and ordered him about just as if he were brain damaged; and still, he said nothing against them nor grew angry at them but merely nodded and sometimes removed his deep blue baseball cap and wiped his moist black forehead with his clean, white handkerchief and then continued on with his slow but steady and efficient labor.

Soon, the students were arriving in their best Sunday-go-to-meeting clothes and the school staff was there and everyone was joyous. The music was good and the food and drink were delicious and the dancing was modest and everyone was delirious with happiness. And then they came.

No one ever knew why they came or what prompted them to come to this town of all towns, but there they were; they just walked right in and immediately everyone there knew that something was absolutely and utterly and completely far off the center of the agreed-upon line of normalcy and decency; in point of fact, they were young hoodlums.

Yes, they were wearing black leather jackets and white t-shirts and blue jeans with the cuffs rolled up and their hair was jet black and combed up and slicked back, and they were, each of the three young men, holding a pint of whiskey.

They appeared on the stage and the leader of the group announced his presence by pulling the trigger of his silver colt .45 and shooting bullets into the high ceiling. The townsfolk stopped what they were doing and stared up at the strangers just as if the sky itself had fallen upon their heads.

"Now, listen up, you stupid hicks, I've got something to say to you," he began in his slurred, sloppy voice, his right hand holding the gun and his left hand holding the amber-colored bottle. "Who do you think you are, having this here dance without inviting me and my boys, huh?" His boys announced their presence by too firing off a round of their handguns into the ceiling. "Got it, pilgrims, you shouldn't have done that, no, you shouldn't have done that bad thing," he shouted, and then his voice seemed to devolve into something meaner and more animal-like, "so I am going to teach you all a lesson in manners," and he pointed the gun at the crowd.

Now, everyone there—the students and staff and guests— were panicking like hens trapped in a pen with a pack of foxes; all of them were, except one, and he merely raised his eyes towards the wooden platform and slowly wiped his forehead and then replaced the handkerchief back into his pocket and retrieved a slick, black bullets-in-the-chamber Walther PPK and with one continuous and seamless motion, just as if he were wiping a dirty window, proceeded to aim that wicked piece of mechanical wizardry right at the targets on stage and then easily pulled the trigger once, sending a 7.65 mm bullet tumbling towards the ring leader, who was about to fire randomly into the audience; and then he distributed his second shot and third shot by imperceptibly moving his gun hand to the right, towards the second and third of the youths as they too were about to fire indiscriminately into the frozen-solid lambkins who were still staring at the big, dark, glistening eyes of the big, black wolves; and so, one, the big, bad leader fell backward with a great push and plopped down to the freshly mopped and polished tiled floor with a sickening thud; and two, the second assassin was propelled backward to fall near his avowed leader; and three, the third assassin too fell in the same misshapen, bloody heap of his loyal crew.

Now, it must be stated for the record—at least for the unwritten record—that everyone there—at least everyone who was conscious—turned and stared straight at Sam as if truly he were an angel recently arrived from Heaven; and no—no one was talking, no one quite knew what to say, except that the mayor did finally manage to blurt out in a choking voice, "How did you know..."

Sam sort of smiled, and said, matter-of-factly, "Shoot, I'm always packing, you know, it just seems like the right thing to do, considering the times, and everything..."

"But how...?" the mayor let slip past his numb lips.

Sam was wiping off the Walther PPK and blowing the smoke from it, and then said, looking innocently up to his stunned audience, "Special Services, nothing really..." And he replaced the weapon back into the brown leather holster inside of his shirt and went back to cleaning up the spill he had been attending to when all of the ruckus had begun.

The sheriff came and the mayor told him what had happened and the sheriff stared with incredulity at the genteel janitor and, after consulting with the other witnesses, formed an opinion that would define the town soon thereafter; when the official police came from the big city next door, the story they heard involved rival youths shooting at each other and one group escaping into the misty night and the other group escaping into the deep slumber that never ends.

The next day, it was a Saturday, and when Sam came into town, everybody smiled and waved and nodded their head and whispered pleasant things about him; and Sam, well, he too nodded his head and smiled and waved back at them before he went to the general store to buy his goods for the week, and afterwards he drove his beige Chevy lazily down the street towards his humble farm.

At school, the students now became more conscious of cleaning up after themselves and saying "excuse me" when they walked around the janitor, and sometimes they even engaged in conversation with him about school projects or the weather or any interesting event occurring in town, and the janitor would smile politely and listen and engage them in conversation, and when it was all over, he would sometimes wipe his forehead with his white handkerchief, and then go back to work.

Within a month Sam was joining the menfolk in pleasant card games and reminiscing about the war and telling tales about lost buddies and lost sweethearts. The people were amazed that he had stories to tell and had lived a life just like any other man, and he had done it, they now knew, despite no help from anyone in town and practically anywhere else— and sometimes, they now knew, in direct opposition to the will and want of people like them everywhere. And they were truly ashamed.

Three months hence, Sam was coming into town to buy his goods one fine summer day when he noticed that the people were having a parade, a big parade replete with the high school marching band and colorful banners. It is for you, the mayor said, it is for you, he shouted so that everyone there could hear, and so he escorted Sam to the park wherein now stood a bronze statue striking a regal pose and a gaze that looked over the town as if it were the guardian of the people. The statue was of Sam. And then the mayor made a speech that he should have made long ago.

"Sam, we are a Freedom-loving nation, we are, but sometimes we only love the freedoms that we decide are good for us and love those people who we think deserve such freedoms—but by doing so, we exclude too many people; and I say to all of you, to exclude one person from the gift of Freedom and Justice and Equality is a moral crime against humanity; so, we here, Sam Washington, ask you to forgive us our trespasses against you and ask you to open the door for more people like yourself so that we might all know what real Freedom is and why our brothers and sisters died protecting it for us; for a freedom won and then taken from just one man is not a freedom we deserve at all, and to live a life apart from those whom we think are not deserving and whom we are afraid of is to live a life not worth examining. How, then, can we ask for the blessings of God every day if we do not ask for the blessings from God for every one of His creatures? I say to you, citizens, this is an abomination in our Republic and will not stand, not anymore in our little town—no longer will we suffer those who are not like us to a fate worse than ours, for now we shall seek to inherit what our founding fathers wanted us to have—and that is Justice and Equality and the pursuit of Happiness."

The crowd cheered and Sam smiled and the entire populace of one thousand two hundred and thirty-eight people celebrated all that day and not a person or a creature went home before the golden sunset cradled the town in love and joy.

And they all did live happily ever after, for soon, that town and many other towns across the great continent had a sack full of black grains and white grains and brown grains and pierced grains and weirdly attired grains and long-haired grains and tattooed grains, and nobody, but nobody seemed to mind too much anymore.

-Finis-

Love

It was a vigil he had never intended for anyone as beautiful and precious as she; a vigil of fidelity he had once reserved for loved ones who had lived a very long life and who one day would lie down upon a feathery-soft bed as they readied themselves for a better life; a passionate vigil for those who might be hurt and needed solace from him; but he had never meant it for her, no, never, just as no one expects anyone young and strong to wither and die before the bowed figures of their grieving elders.

He was sitting on a small white plastic chair beside her hospital bed, his large hand holding her small hand, his left hand tenderly stroking her wet forehead as he waited for her to awaken from the numbing effects of the powerful pain medication; he had been here for days and was prepared to stay for many more; he had slept little and not eaten the entire time and had drunk only water as he had attended to his precious little one, his own flesh and blood, comforting a mind and body that desired the serenity and calm other good boys and girls around the world have.

"Daddy," she murmured now, as his child returned from the land of sweet slumber, "Daddy, where are you?"

He had been stimulated in all his senses when she had awoken and spoken his name, but when she asked where he was, he felt a horrific helplessness eat away at his internal courage. "I'm here, darling; your Daddy is here," he whispered, and he massaged her soaked, long brown hair. "I'm here, Evelyn—your Daddy is always here for you."

When she opened her tired eyes to reveal the still-glorious radiance that is youth—an iridescent crown of dark brown set in a rich sea of luminous snow white—he felt the villainy of cruel fate stab his heart. She should live, he thought, she who is so young still, so unspoiled; and then he bent over and tenderly kissed her warm forehead.

"Daddy," she whispered, in a weak voice, "I dreamed of Mommy, and Mommy held me, and she said she loved me, and she loved you, too."

He felt his feeble, mortal body fail as she spoke thus, and he wanted to weep, but held it back with great resolve. "Yes, Evelyn, you had a beautiful dream, and I am so very glad you saw Mommy."

"Daddy, how much do you miss Mommy?"

"Oh, Evelyn," he whispered, his voice devoured by burning pathos, "I miss her so very much."

She smiled and uttered a small giggle. "Daddy," she said, holding out her hands, "you look so handsome in your curly brown beard."

The tears held back so long began to cast their appeal to slide down his pale cheeks, but he fought hard to rein them in as he leaned forward and felt her small fingers caress his whiskered face. I want to remember all of this, he thought, as he beheld her wondrous, innocent smile; I want to savor every moment of this, for one day there will be no other moments...

Her soft visage became tense when the malevolent spirit of searing pain visited her once more; but then she managed to say, as she beheld his worried expression, "Daddy, I will be your brave little girl."

He held her tiny hand now in both of his hands as he lifted them up and kissed the top of them. "You are my brave little girl, the bravest little girl in the whole wide world."

"Daddy," she said, curiously, "you have told me there are other sick little girls like me."

"Yes, sweetheart."

"And are their parents with them?"

"Yes, darling."

"And are these little girls brave, too?"

He expelled a short breath as he nodded. "Yes, they are brave, too."

She knit her blonde eyebrows. "I wish I knew them too, Daddy, I wish I could be friends with them; I think they are as brave as me, 'specially if they have their Mommy and Daddy with them."

He smiled at her goodness. "Yes, Evelyn."

"I'm glad they are brave, and have their Mommy and Daddy with them—and maybe brothers and sisters, too; I will see them in Heaven, won't I?"

"Yes," he returned, and then felt the presence of sorrow grow in his heart, for to utter such an affirmation meant he had acquiesced to the inevitable outcome of her stay in this sterile institution—something he knew would occur but had refused to acknowledge.

"Mommy is waiting for me in Heaven, too, isn't she, Daddy?"

"Yes, darling," he said, softly, holding her hand again and stroking her moist hair and forehead.

"I am not afraid to go to Heaven—Jesus will hold my hand until I get there, won't he, Daddy?"

"Yes, baby, He will be there for you."

"I love Jesus, Daddy, and I love Mommy—I will tell that to them when I see them in Heaven...Daddy?"

"Yes, my precious darling."

"I love you, Daddy, I love you so much, and am so very proud of you, and I will tell Mommy how much you still love her when I see her."

You mustn't cry, he scolded himself, not now; if you start now you will never stop and she will see you as weak—you must be strong for her, now.

Their inviolate love for each other, this unconditional, simple, precious love between father and daughter, constructed a window of pure white light through which they could peer into the natural soul of the other, where there are no secrets a good father and good daughter keep from each other.

She closed her eyes and squeezed them tight as the pain throttled her, and her small form, dressed in white cotton robes, rose up in tense spasms; warm tears ran down her flushed cheeks and were soon wiped away by the gentle, warm hand of her father; when the mighty turbulence had passed through her, she opened her eyes, her breath still quick; and she assembled a weak smile as she looked to the only human being left for her to love. "It doesn't hurt much, Daddy," she whispered, as she squeezed his hand, "I'll be all right," and as she held her head askew, a quizzical look came upon her face; "is there pain in Heaven, Daddy?"

"No, Evelyn, no pain at all," he said, shaking his head; and then he quoted, "and every tear shall be wiped away." And then he smiled and whispered with great affection, "You are the bravest little daughter," and he closed his eyes, "Mommy would be so proud."

Her face was illuminated by Love and Joy. "Would she, Daddy, do you really think so?"

"I know so, Evelyn—she used to say so, so very often," he murmured, nodding his head, and then, thinking that very soon he would utter her blessed name and there would be no reply, he felt his heart shudder, and his soul felt the terrible pang of emptiness and loneliness seize him and begin to reshape him into their suffering image.

She nodded to her father, to her lifeline, to the only human being through whom she now interpreted the world; and then she smiled, as if to reassure the man whom she knew loved her so very much, a love she felt covering her like a soft, lamb-wool blanket, and then said with great certitude in her voice, "I am not afraid, Daddy."

"I know you are not, Evelyn," he whispered, smiling too as he still held her hand.

"I will tell Mommy that you love her so very much." A rippling, cutting pain tore up and down her body, and as she stiffened, a small wail of agony escaped her pale lips.

He could feel the sensation of weeping enlarging itself in him, and still, he held back its awesome fury; and then he said, as he leaned forward and placed his arms around her, "I am going with you, sweetheart."

Even though the pain was slowly retreating in her, she still managed to say, "Oh, Daddy, you can't come with me, silly!"

He barely shook his head. "I am coming with you, my beautiful little angel."

The pain had fallen and so she relaxed, and then she opened her eyes; and she whispered to him, just as if she were not in any agony at all, "Daddy, do you love me?" But she was not looking at him now.

He sat back down, still holding her hand. "Yes, darling, I love you so very much."

"Daddy, do you love me?" she whispered again, still not looking at him, and now in a very mature voice that bespoke wisdom beyond her years.

He felt panic usurp his fragmented strength as he said, "Yes, baby, I love you more than anything in this whole wide world." He reached now into his pants pocket and retrieved a blue pill and surreptitiously placed it into his mouth.

But now she looked directly at him and her face was full of calm, and her smile was unrestrained. "Daddy, do you love me and Mommy?"

"Yes, Evelyn, I love you and Mommy so very much."

Her head bent slightly now as she looked upon him. "Daddy, Daddy, you must stay here, to help other little sick children like me."

He shook his head, the emotional pain of denying the request of the only human being who was still part of him weighing him down just as if a large stone had been placed upon his mortal head; and he spoke softly and gently, as if to lighten the hurt of his denial to her. "I cannot, Evelyn, I cannot."

She smiled once more, just as if the omnipresent pain in her was at abeyance now. "Daddy, promise me you will stay and help them."

His puny defenses against the overwhelming presence of sobbing within him were weakening fast, as he had fewer and fewer real obstacles to throw up against it now; and then he said, his voice cracking now, with little resolve, "Baby, I can't; I want to go with you so we can be a family again."

"No, Daddy, no," she murmured, reaching out her small hand to caress his wet brown hair as his head fell next to her frail body. "Mommy and I will be so very proud of you if you stay here and help little children like me."

He was sobbing now, for he had capitulated to the ready forces of sorrow and grief, and he allowed them to fully command his senses and emotions; and so when he spoke, his voice was pathos unrestrained. "I just can't, Evelyn, I don't want to stay here all alone; please don't ask me, please, Evelyn, my little angel, please, please, I want so very much to be with you and Mommy in Heaven."

"Promise me, Daddy, please promise me, won't you," she said, with great affection, as she stroked his long, brown, curly hair, "that you will stay here and help little children like me get well." She heard his mild protestations once more, and once more she said, in a soothing, gentle tone, "You are my Daddy, and a good, good man, Mommy told me so; you are the best Daddy, and I will see you in Heaven soon; but now, please, Daddy, will you stay and help little children like me so they can stay with their Mommy and Daddy—and maybe their brothers and sisters—if they have them, and be a family like our family?"

He knew from the moment she asked this question that he could not deny her. "Yes, yes, Evelyn, my beautiful and good daughter," he whispered, nodding as he raised a face that was awash with pious tears, "I will stay and help little children like you so they can stay here with their mothers and fathers—and brothers and sisters—if they have them," and he reached out his hand and stroked her sweaty temple and the side of her warm face, "to grow up straight and tall and true, just like you would want them to be."

"I am so proud of you, Daddy," she whispered, "I have always been so very proud of you." She closed her eyes. "I am dreaming now, Daddy."

He removed the blue pill from his mouth and placed it back into his pocket.

"I am dreaming of Heaven now, Daddy."

"Yes, darling," he said, still weeping, his head lifted up now, and he kissed her warm forehead and warm cheeks as he held her close.

"I love you so very much, Daddy," she said, smiling as a radiant shine came to her smooth face, "I love you so very much, Mommy; I love you so very much, Jesus—take my hand."

Then there was an absolute stillness all about him now, as if the world had stopped moving; as if the heartbeat of humanity had halted and taken note and lamented the loss of one so pure and innocent and full of grace; and then he unhooked the long tubes and the electronic wires from her and took her in his arms and gently rocked her to and fro just as she had liked it not too very long ago.

It wasn't too much time later—as the march of time is recorded in the annals of history—that two nurses were standing near their workstation, discussing their patients, when an elderly, white-haired doctor came walking down the white-tiled, glossy hallway in front of them.

A sense of awe encompassed them, as if they had been suddenly transported into another dimension—a princely domain they were honored to attend.

The nurse with the blonde hair crossed her arms and whispered to her companion, "Have you seen him before?"

"No," whispered the redheaded nurse, whose bare arms hung helplessly at her sides, "but I get butterflies just seeing him."

The blonde-haired nurse smiled. "He's really a sweet man, especially for someone so important."

The redhead said, still whispering, "He discovered the cure for Acute Lymphoblastic Leukemia, and still he works in the Children's Cancer Ward—I mean, he could be sailing on a yacht, drinking margaritas…"

The blonde-haired woman laughed, as her friend shrunk down in embarrassment. "You don't know him like we do—that just isn't his style—and if you knew why he worked so hard all those years for the cure…" She smiled in fond remembrance. "This is his yacht."

"I heard it was because of his little girl."

"Yes, it was for her—and his wife had died shortly before her, too—and he never remarried, and went to medical school and graduated with top honors; and then found the cure, and even now he is working on other cures, too." She smiled that sort of smile one assumes when a pleasant thought occurs that is noble in its nature and imparts virtue to the one who devised it. "Can you imagine a world without people such as he?"

Her friend, upon hearing such a query, and then recognizing its pernicious assault upon the fragile universe, shook her head as tears welled up in her eyes; and yea, she attempted to speak, but an imagined fear sealed it shut.

The two friends watched in silence as a new patient was wheeled into the Children's Cancer Ward; and they watched how, with great solicitude, the white-bearded doctor bent down and shook the hand of the young girl and welcomed her with a warm smile and a wink and a hearty hello, and then stood up and shook the hands of her parents and then personally showed them to the child's new room; and presently he came back, and slowly walked up to the two nurses, and introduced himself to the new nurse with a gentle smile and a firm handshake, and told her how happy he was to meet her and how honored he was to have her on the staff of the hospital; and then presently he walked down the hallway to check on the other patients he considered not only his patients but patients of the world; whom he considered not only his children, but children of the world; whose future he considered but also considered the future of the world: to be cared for by him, and by their families and neighbors and friends, until the terrible disease they had was banished from little boys and girls the world over.

-Finis-

The Whispering Bells

They had small bodies with teeny tiny little legs and teeny tiny little arms and a head shaped just like yours and mine and a face with eyes and nose and mouth too, but they wore an expression upon it that was not like yours and mine. They were the Whispering Bells.

They did not call themselves the Whispering Bells, but that is how it all comes out when their language is translated into ours. It is not a very good rendering because their name changed wherever they went and whenever they did something, and if the place they went to was spectacular and the something they did was fantastic, then their new name stayed longer with them. But perhaps it is best now to begin at the beginning and tell you how they came to help us write our own history.

They lived long ago, and not on some planet or meteoroid or even an asteroid, even though some scholars have theorized that this was possible; for, you see, they lived in the free, boundless regions of outer space, traveling the galaxies and going where their fancies took them. They never worried about home or hearth or food or drink, for the black void of the cosmos was their only home, and the drifting gas and dust that circulated throughout the universe was their nourishment as it sifted through their porous bodies.

They did not have an oral language, but they had the special language of the stars and the intimate language their bodies evinced when they wished to communicate to each other. It was when they flew—their bodies able to absorb solar winds for flight—that they were the most content, flying with their postures erect and their faces flush with the fervor of hope and joy and their arms held straight out above their heads and their feet close together; and when they soared within the majestic borders of the kaleidoscope of rainbow-colored auroras with the music of the firmament flowing into them, they were at their happiest.

A primordial song flowed throughout the universe as cosmic radiation, which the Bells assimilated into their entire bodies, thus allowing them to experience its full spectrum of octaves and decibels and harmonies and melodies; now, this music must not be thought of as the kind of artificial music we humans compose, which is based on mammon or emotion, but a completely unpretentious and nonlinear symphony that is the ripples of sound which have emerged from the exotic embryo wherefrom came time and space. The sublime rivers and streams of this clean and crisp and clear music were as vital for the Bells as were their food and flying.

The Whispering Bells swam through the swirling aurora galaxilis the same way fish swim through our flowing ocean depths, and there was an infinite variety of these ambling lights throughout the universe; some were as big as the highest mountain and some as small as the tiniest seed, ever moving, ever dancing, ever present; and all of them had an inexhaustible amount of colors—mustard yellow and shocking pink and marine green in one layer, which might spread out in a wide arc, and raspberry purple and periwinkle blue and pumpkin orange in another layer, which might fly out in a tight pattern—two patterns that might slowly interweave and caress each other and then move on to another pattern and a different point in space. There were concentric circles of these colors collapsing upon each other and then regrouping to form new patterns that darted and dived together like birds of the air, and prismatic shapes and radial shapes and conical shapes, cubed shapes and diamond shapes and branched shapes, and wheel shapes and vortex shapes and spinning shapes, and spherical shapes and saucer shapes and stellar shapes; and any geometric shape the world has ever experienced, but even a few more that the world will never experience because it lost its innocence long ago, when it lay down with lust and greed.

The Whispering Bells followed the auroras like nomads following herds of game. Now, when they entered into the body of the dazzling lights, they went singly or in pairs, as too many together in the tears of creation could not properly achieve serenity and solace therein; so, when they did go inside, they did so with their minds free of dismay and disunity, for their minds had to be in tune with the rhythm of Nature.

And when their lithe forms entered into the coiled and spiraled, stripy, dotted and horizontal, elliptical, vertical and crisscrossed patterns, when they rode on the reticular and piped, variegated, ringed and ribbed, curved, zigzagged and waffled styles, when they turned up and over and found an inner groove on the checkered and fretted, argyle, damascened and vermiculated, banded, stippled and speckled structures, they were in a state of soaring and secure bliss, for here was the life breath of the heavens, the deft paintbrush of time, the mural of Nature, unspoiled, untouched and unadorned; and as the Bells too experienced the exquisite space music inside this nurturing cocoon, they thrived like a newborn baby in the tender arms of its mother.

It was the sacred duty of every Bell to protect and defend their own and any life-form that was defenseless or needed succor; they treated every member of their race as family, and in this way, equality and justice reigned supreme. They had no rulers or judges, no police or prisons, and the only law that governed them stated that if any Bell committed an act of violence against another of its own kind, it would be banished forever. They had no ambition other than to live freely so they might be free to pursue and embrace joy.

When they were not surfing the rising and falling waves of auroras that tunneled and spun their way through the frozen galaxies, the Bells were riding piggyback on speeding asteroids and meteoroids, inspecting planets and comets, and discovering new things to play with. Many of the Bells were expert in manipulating meteors into other meteors to create fantastic collisions, and sometimes they even directed big asteroids into planets, to watch the giant explosions that were made upon impact.

One of their favorite games occurred every time the meteoroid family came round to their vicinity: every Bell, male and female, young and old, would form two long, parallel lines that seemed to stretch for miles, and then they would watch the daring young males and females on their flying trapezes.

A small meteoroid would come streaking down between the two rows of Bells and one of the youths would fly to and mount it like a rider on horseback. One particular time a young female, Popcorn Flower, whose body was a mash of mellow yellow and powder blue, flew alongside a jagged piece of meteoroid and reached out her hands and grasped it and began to twirl about until she was just a magnificent

blur of vibrant green. The Bells cheered. Then came a bigger
chunk of rock and, naturally, a male Bell flew to its side—
Kinnikinnick was his name, a fine fellow with bright streaks
of rose red and beryl green—and first he mounted the jagged
piece of free real estate backward, eliciting much applause
from his audience; he then turned round, and as he rode this
piece of ancient history, he began to spin and spin so swiftly
that soon he gave off a blush of charming yellow. Next, one
of the more daring of the females, Wild Candytuft, who was
brushed beautifully and symmetrically with deep blues and
reds, flew into the lane and caught a lumpy, pitted rock and
went ahead of it and began to twirl, and as she did so, she gave
off brilliant sparks of majestic magenta, and then she slowed
down and somersaulted up and over and onto the meteoroid
and raised her hands in glee. Oh, how the Bells roared their
silent approval!

Now, it must be stated here that the most daring of all the
maneuvers on the meteoroids involved steering them toward
planets, a very dangerous affair for the Bells, for it had been
recorded in their history that some of them had long ago
crashed with the rocks into such places, and that, according to
legend, some Bells had fallen with the stone ponies into these
worlds, which had some outer barrier that caused the rocks
to slow and burn—a place, some said, where Bells could not
fly—and because of this, Mother Bells and Father Bells were
very strict in not allowing their Baby Bells to fly too close to
the surface of these drifting celestial bodies.

Ah, but the far reach of parents did not put a hold on
the Bell youths, who, just as our youths do here, incessantly
engage in feats of bravado to prove themselves to their peers.

The next performer for the lane on this day was Firecracker
Flower, a most rambunctious male youth who was always

going where he was not supposed to go, and doing what he was not supposed to do; here, then, came a rather large, misshapen, craggy piece of meteoroid, and its raggedy appearance appealed to him; so he came directly to it, and with his bright streaks of magenta and cyan, mounted it and quickly directed it toward the forbidden zone.

The elder Bells gasped and the youths squealed in excitement as they watched the wild rider bear down on the space horse and speed toward the planet; and as he did so, friction began to pummel the rock and flames began to fly off it, but Firecracker Flower, immune to fire, as were all the Bells, held on fast, his form giving off deep shades of blue; but when the rock was beginning to disintegrate, Firecracker Flower let go and turned round and flew upward and back into the safety of space, all to the great and enthusiastic applause of the Bells.

Sun Rose, a female youth with equal amounts of delicious red and cyan and green saturating her lithe body, flew next into the arena and easily caught a rock and steered it into the planet and she too held on fast as the rock burned and her form gave off a luminous, sparkly white, and then she let go as the meteoroid began to dissolve, and then she turned round and flew back up into space and accepted her hearty applause. Then came Blazing Star.

Blazing Star was as reckless a youth as there was amongst the Bells; if there was a comet his elders begged him not to explore, he explored it; and if there was an unknown territory of the cosmos, such as the esoteric Angel Trumpets, with its eerie and frightening noises emerging from bubbling, swirling, sooty vapors, he would go there.

So, here was Blazing Star, proudly wearing his patches of dazzling yellow and magenta, grabbing hold of a slab of slick meteoroid rock and maneuvering it straight into the cauldron of the unexpected, and upon entering into the thin atmosphere, he held on tight as his body gave off a pulse of cherry red; and soon the rising flames encircled him and the meteor broke apart, but still he held on tight, tighter and tighter, long past the time when he should have let go had he wished to be perfectly safe; but no, he was a youth who lived for the thrill of challenging the esoteric, and when he finally did let go and turned to fly up toward the now faraway black horizon, he felt a strange power ebb, as if he could no longer manage flight; but in a moment this flux was gone and he was in full flight and strength again, and he soon swooped in front of the crowd to great applause. He wanted to tell someone about the strange effect he had felt on his powers but he quickly decided that it would diminish his glory, and so he simply took his place in line and anxiously awaited the next contestant.

The Coral Bells were next, sisters and twins and drenched in swirls of yellow and cyan, and they found two small meteoroids and flew to them and danced around them and twirled about them until their bodies gave off a lovely shade of green, and then they flew away and bowed before the pleased audience. After this, there were many more such acts, brothers and sisters, entire families, tumbling and spinning about and on top of the black, craggy meteoroids, and the Bells loved it all, loved every moment of the acrobatic flights and the colorful displays and the wondrously choreographed dancing.

It was, curiously, never over until it was over, which is to say that sometimes these celebrations went on for a very long time, and even when it appeared that there were no more volunteers, another Bell stepped in—and this time his name was Sky Pilot, and he was cloaked in bolts of raspberry red and canary yellow.

His two older brothers had performed before him and dazzled the crowd with their fine athleticism, and he decided that it was his time to shine, and because of this, he would become the most famous of all the Bells.

Here came a rather ordinary-looking meteoroid with dull edges and chips and dents, but Sky Pilot flew to it and grasped it and immediately made his intent clear: he was going straight into the heart of the planet below. So, there he took the captured rock and he held it fast and low as it sank into the upper atmosphere and encountered friction and his body flashed tangerine orange; the rock began to burn and quake, but Sky Pilot would not relent; and when the rock began to flame up and disintegrate, he would still not relent; and when the rock began to crumble and split apart, he finally let go and turned upward to fly away back to space.

But his power was gone.

His flying ability was a flicker now, and like a flickering candle, it soon went out, and as he began to fall, he could see the faint images of dark space above him slowly disappear until nothing remained but a hazy, blotchy, foggy soup of gray, and as he fell further, he saw the heavens open up and he was immersed in a sea of cerulean beauty. In the next moment, he slammed into the hard surface.

He was not hurt because his body had slowed tremendously due to the wondrous air on this young planet. He slowly stood up and looked round to see a landscape of barren rock and plumes of steam rising from its core. Bells could walk when they needed to, and so Sky Pilot began to wander about, looking for signs of life but finding none. He knew he was alone.

Still, he was young, and optimism drove him onward to search this boiling wilderness, and soon he found himself experiencing a sensation he had never known—hunger. But what was there to do but move on, and he continued to wander about the place, occasionally looking up to the gorgeous azure sky with a sad, forlorn face.

He soon fell asleep, and when he awoke, he was frightened, for all about him was sunlight, and his eyes could not tolerate the brightness. But then something touched him.

He rose up, his eyes shielded by his arms, and he felt the touch of a hand caressing his head and gently pulling him, and although he became fearful, he decided to follow. In a little while he was led into a cave and there he opened his eyes and beheld a creature just like himself—a female Bell, and as lovely as any other he had ever seen. She was awash in iridescent colors of purple and red, and gorgeous green and orange, and she even had a streak of scintillating silver weaving its way down her slender frame. Her name was Globe Flower, and he was enraptured by her beauty.

She introduced him to her family with the intricate gestures all the Bells used to communicate with each other, and soon, she told him how she and her family had come to be here.

A very long time ago, she began, a Bell family had ventured too near this fire planet and had been captured by it the same way Sky Pilot had been; so they had set out to explore their new home and soon found forms of food, which they learned how to feed into their bodies. They found these caves to dwell in, and after a few generations, were able to withstand the intense light, allowing them to travel where they pleased. Even their colors changed, and she gestured, smiling, toward her rainbow-colored kin.

That night, Globe Flower took Sky Pilot on a journey, and when they approached their destination, she made him cover his eyes, and then had him put a foot into the crystal-blue sea. He jerked it away and opened his eyes and turned round and tried to fly but only succeeded in falling helplessly to the ground. Globe Flower was much amused, and soon dived into the pristine, warm waters and swam about, beckoning him to come to her. He eventually did, after much teasing from her, but he would only wade in a little bit and then jump out and then wade in again and jump out again. Globe Flower smiled and clapped.

On their way back to the caves, she showed him the home of the Silky Beach Peas, a tiny group of wayfarers who had been marooned on this bleak island for centuries. Sky Pilot bent down and stared at the mass of metallic-colored orbs that grew hotter whenever his hand neared them, and grew icy cold whenever his hand pulled away from them; they looked like a group of marbles, of clearies and steelies and aggies, and there was one that was colored the darkest shade of winter, which turned into a bubbling mass of lava and rose like the whirling vortex of a tornado when Sky attempted to touch it, and when he took his hand away, it regained its original shape; and there was another that was colored the lightest tint of creamy yellow, and when he put his hand near it, it transformed into a miniature sun and gave forth such a luminous light that he had to turn his face away, and when he looked again, the creamy yellow orb was there once more. There were also the False Baby Stars, who were balls of wispy threads of light that produced a small, tinkling noise, and when he approached them, they seared their way into the rock and tunneled until they popped out some safe distance away. There were diverse colonies of creatures all up and down the rocky, gouged and boiling beach, and together with Globe Flower, he would discover them all.

Soon, Sky would go into the sea without fear, and learn to pour and rub the thick, oozing soup Globe Flower gave him against his body to rid himself of hunger, and adjust to the weird sensation of noise, and learn to tolerate the light, and learn to love Globe Flower and her kin.

But the Bells in space were horrified that one of their own had not come back from this robbing sphere, and thus resolved that they would rescue him; and so, for a long time they searched the traveling meteoroids and asteroid belts and the comet clusters for a suitable candidate for their plan, and even braved passing near the dreaded ebony mists of the Angel Trumpets, and flew close to the oscillating, flashing lights of the Golden Fairy Lantern region, and even busted right through the thick clouds known as the Fairy Dusters; but they eventually did find one, far, far away, and soon they began to usher it back toward the area where Sky Pilot had fallen.

It was as big as a small planet, the kind of asteroid they might have played on in happier times, but now they would use its great mass to accomplish their mission; and so, with every Bell behind the immense rock, every Bell young and old, weak and strong, male and female, they began to push against it with all of their strength, pushing and pushing it toward this blue globe that had stolen their own. Now, it must not be supposed that this took a little time, no indeed, for to alter the course of such a grotesquely huge object not only took great effort but occurred over a great period of time. Eventually, the pockmarked, gray asteroid was aligned with the planet, and the Bells pushed with all of their might and flew with all of their strength and soon it was within the atmosphere below and the Bells let go, exhausted.

Sky Pilot and Globe Flower were playing in the sparkling seas when they looked up and saw the immense object fall in the far distance. A great explosion occurred and they were bounced and shaken about for the longest time as great plumes of vapor and fire roared up into the sky; and when finally Sky Pilot looked up, he was back in outer space but still on land, which was now a huge chunk of wounded rock that floated above the planet below. He rushed to Globe Flower and held her in his arms and watched her small body simply stop all its life processes.

He mourned her death, and when he went back to the cave, he mourned the death of her kin.

He had the ability to fly again but he did not leave this new satellite, not until the Bells came and found him and rejoiced at his safety; and even then, he was reluctant to leave Globe Flower, and stayed by her side for the longest time.

The orbiting hunk of rock would gain more meteoroid hits, as would the wounded planet below, quite often meteoroids directed by the Bells, but mostly directed by Nature. Today, we look up at this bright structure that sits like an abandoned child in the icy grip of lonely space, and wonder what life might have occupied it, and truly, where it came from.

The history of the Whispering Bells is a history that few people have ever heard of, and it is a history that can only be found in the most secret of places and by the most special of people; and so, if you are that very special person and happen to go to that very special place and read about the adventures of this ancient race, you must then decide whom to share this sacred text with; for every time a special person hears it, tiny fragments of its history come together and become clearer, but every time a not-so-special person hears it, tiny fragments of the history of the Whispering Bells melt away forever into the darkest, most unfathomable oblivion.

-Finis-

Crashing Into You

We may seek to walk paths strictly parallel to each other for all our long lives in order to avoid the confusion and upheaval of one another, but inevitably, as we travel over this green and blue planet, our paths do cross; and only then is there human chaos and social advancement; and who are the victors, and who are the vanquished?

She was driving as if she had lived a thousand thrilling lifetimes, as if oblivious and unsympathetic to her environs and wearing a cloak of invincibility that had formed at her marvelous birth; no one living and no wise script from the past could dissuade her to slow from the frenetic pace she pursued down any street, highway or byway; no amount of lecturing, no role model, no friends or family, no one at all, could alter her fantastic commingling of unbound speed and fury down any road, boulevard and bridge, for she was the crowned queen of freedom that was gained only when the outer limits of society's strictest rules were shattered again and again and in every way imaginable and unimaginable.

Her skills of maneuverability were beyond compare and intruding into a higher echelon wherein only the finest and most adroit pilots of derring-do existed; so, as she was beautiful, she was arrogant; and as she was fiery young, so unassumingly and alarmingly young, so uncontrollably and indefinably and indescribably young, she believed in eternity—and certainly the epic eternity of her radiant youth, bought and fulfilled by an exuberant energy and ability to prevail against disease, death and destruction.

In her youthful mind, if her car chanced to hit a wall of any great proportion or density, she would merely bounce off it as simply as a red rubber ball bounces harmlessly off a red brick wall, whereafter her body would merely reform as easily and naturally as that ball—a small impression upon her person that would soon inflate and return to normal and plunge once more back onto the black leather seat of her magical pirate ship.

Did the serpentine roads offer a sharp curve to her? She pressed her bare bronze feet with even more vigor upon the custom-made, grey metallic accelerator pedal of her cherry-red 1970 Mach 1 Ford Mustang with its magnificent horsepower, and increased her white and toothy grin even wider; did the open road suggest a tamer speed around sheer mountain cliffs? She only opened up the throttle even more and opened up her carmine lips and laughed even harder; did the highway allow for a greater latitude for speed? Why, she merely threw back her blonde, curly head and punched the shaped-like-a-foot pedal and roared like the great blue blazes until no black and white cruiser, except a black and white helicopter, could catch her—and it did not matter if she was eventually stopped by a highway patrol officer who said he had clocked her at one hundred sixty miles per hour, because she had only to proffer him that sensuous, pouting smile and allow her round head to rest askew as she gazed up at the poor trapped-like-a-rab-bit-in-her-magnificent-headlights male, with her scintillating powder-blue eyes and her bronze, fit body tilted up at him with its affectionate, come-hither posture and her honey-scented perfume wafting around him like perfume from a blossoming apple tree, and he was slayed, thereby; so she was a free spirit once more—and one recognized by the male officer, too—a primal, natural woman who lives in all women but who is dulled and shaved to anonymity by the rigors and conventions of modernity; a fierce creature the officer intrinsically identified with and longed to see wild and free to roam without the tired shackles of tired rules that restricted her adventurous nature in any direction she desired; and into that direction she would magnify the warmth and brightness of the sun and illuminate the liquid golden crown of dawn and cause all raggedy things to appear new and all crooked things to seem straighter and all dimmed things to acquire a deep, radiant luster; and when she had discharged all of her narcotic pheromones into the face of the limp officer, she drove away from the scene triumphant and more emboldened.

Thus, her ebullient fires were daily stoked by men, who worshipped her natural and rare beauty, and by women, who admired her independent and radical nature; she was an electrically charged super body, allowed to spin her own fast way and do as she pleased without ever once considering the possibility of failure and its terrible consequences—just as an ignited rocket that flies high up into the thin atmosphere and explodes into a glittery rainbow firework and crashes down on anyone and anything laments only its own fiery passing.

So, there our fearless heroine went, tearing down multitudinous paths, confident, laughing and boasting; and there she journeyed down the small beach-town streets, her bullet-like car a vanilla-crème-colored blur; and her effect upon gawking men was to cleanly rip out their bulging hearts and put these beating muscles into a glass jar that she kept between her long, supple legs.

The day was young and the clear sky was royal blue and painted in broad strokes of white spirals and puffy marshmallow clouds; it was a day of dreamy wonderings and pastoral realities, when Man is a vessel through which Nature pours out her richest bouquet of bounties, when Man breathes in the affection of clean, pure breezes and tastes the pride and majesty of life's vital forces, where all things that are bad and perilous and daunting are rendered good and harmless and easily overcome; it was on this princely day, a gorgeous, awakening spring day, when she, that paradigm of temptation, Lucille Elizabeth Vargas, was, as they say, tooling down an empty street, just as if she were not the sole driver on this quiet road but a driver all others in town needed to heed and admire as she shot by; well, this time she was quietly cranking that 351 Cleveland engine through its high-performance gears, and she thrust her head back and felt the warm wind blow through her long, blonde hair and caress her bare, bronze shoulders; she smiled as she felt the abrupt impact of power envelop her strong, curvaceous body; she was a baby now inside the safe womb of her nurturing mother, and she felt that no harm might visit her nor cause harm to others, for she was merely in the proper place doing the proper thing, as she felt compelled to do by her majestic nature; she was more than a mere operator of a high-performance automobile that had a combustible engine and fuel injection system and four one-thousand-dollar tires: she was like a pioneering argonaut, an aeronaut, an astronaut, an autonaut sailing across the open asphalt seas in search of adventure and satisfaction.

But then there was the curious appearance of the man—he seemed to come through a split in the time-space continuum and just materialize right there upon the now-crunching and quickly cracked windshield; and then, with one terrific and hideous-sounding bounce, he seemed to vanish from sight.

She had a bewildered look upon her luscious face as she pondered this phantasmagoria; had it really happened, she thought, her blonde, arched, thin eyebrows knit; and upon seeing evidence of no one around, she decided it perhaps had been a flux in the wind, a meandering bolt of distorted vision temporarily clogging her keen eyesight; but as her attention turned straight ahead once more, her still-stable mind toured the obvious physical markings in the curved glass before her, and she cocked her head and finally let go of the deep plunge her bare foot had on the pedal, and she instinctively looked in the right rearview mirror and saw a commotion therein; and so, still thinking herself quite innocent of any connection to this scene behind her, she quickly pulled aside to the white cement curb; and exiting the car, she saw many people rushing to a certain spot, to which she too rushed; and as she got there, she observed, as surely as if she were watching this macabre vision through a large telescope, a man down.

A man was down, surely, and he was in terrible pain, undeniably, and writhing about in his death throes and screaming for mercy—and then he absolutely, and without announcement, expired; and just at that moment, all of the people there, lo, even the smallest child to the oldest adult, as if their necks were built upon one common and well-oiled swivel, turned their hard stares against the audacious opinion that was named Miss Autonaut; and their hands, as if too in magical connection with one another, lifted up slowly and pointed with certainty, and clarity, directly at her; and lo, a tiny voice, emitted from a tiny child, spoke, as if in her immature language there was now planted the eternal harvest of Justice: "She did it."

It made no sense for Lucille, the unbound speeder, the fearless Rita-Racer extraordinaire, to hear this than it would for a renowned and highly skilled surgeon to hear accusations that she had deliberately or even carelessly mutilated a patient; she merely shook her head—and her entire intellect shook, too, and her shallow cast of emotions with it, as a tepid "No" crept through her thin, sensuous lips—denial incarnate. "No," she whispered again, as if it were necessary, upon a viewing of the fresh corpse of the first negative uttered, to clearly enunciate her obvious defense again; but she no longer spoke to a phalanx of separate entities but a newly emerging creature that breathed in disdain and exhaled venom—its inbred kin being the Human Gang, the Mob, the soul of unfettered Riot and its cool and cunning inbred cousin, Madness—Swarm Intelligence.

But now lumbering down the road came the ubiquitous black and white symbol to divide this gathering storm into tiny, insignificant droplets of least resistance, thus rendering them powerless; it was the blaring siren, first, then the car arriving, next; then the two burly men encroaching upon this stirring, last; there was an easily acknowledged acceding of the crowd to relinquish its mystical power, to relax its sanguinary bite of the big, black wolf's jaws and allow the receding of toxic tide of animus and vengeance that had seeped out of its stinging, wet pores.

And what of Miss Hot Pants, Miss Rocket Foot, she who will never die nor cause the death of any Innocent despite her most irresponsible circus-on-the-road, flying-woman-on-a-vehicular-trapeze, push-absurdity-to-the-limit act? She was wholly incapable of assembling the required parts of the visual and auditory puzzle presented before her so she might process the meaning and context of the dazzling context; she who was hitherto untouchable was now touched, and she was undone.

* * * * *

What was the young and handsome and very burly officer saying to her, she wondered now as she was escorted, somewhat unaffectionately—it was curious to her for a man to put his arms around her without exceeding affection—to the squad car; what did he say, she pondered after the other officer had inspected her car and walked up and down the unsettling scene while examining the distance with his keen eyes and using a metallic measuring tape at various points on the road; and what is that ambulance doing here, she wondered, is someone hurt?—oh my gosh, I hope someone didn't die—how awful! And what did the officer who came back from his brief interviews with witnesses say to her—it was all so confusing, really; where are they taking me, she thought, what have I done? Are we going to a masquerade party? I don't get it, I really don't.

She tried to focus her mind on it all but met only a thick, sooty bank of cold, drifting fog.

What is this silvery metallic bracelet I am wearing now—don't they know it is not in fashion—why are we driving past my car, my beautiful car—why is it being hoisted upon that tow truck? Am I to drive this car? When have I ever been in the backseat of a car—oh, how funny—I don't think I have ever been in the backseat except to—well, where am I now? How did we get here so quickly? What did that mean, ol' fat woman in the green uniform say to me? I have to submit to what? Where am I now?—what is this place—these steel bars—is this the party we were going to—then who are all these girls in this dirty, cold place with me? What is happening to me? What have I done? And where is my car? Oh, I just want to get in my car and drive home and crawl into bed and pull the covers over me and go to sleep and wake up and then—poof—all gone, bye-bye, bad dream!

Where am I now? Why are these ugly ol' women escorting me into this large room with all these rude people staring at me? Why am I still wearing this awful orange uniform? Who is that man in the black robe behind that big bench? Why is he talking that way to me? He reminds me of what my father might have looked like—plead, plead to what? Someone, someone, somewhere, please, please, please, tell me what I have done wrong—Mommy, please help me!

Now I am in my best clothes and my mommy and best friends in the whole wide world are sitting behind me and everything is going to be all right now, I just know it; the nice woman who sits next to me in the pretty dress will say nice things about me to the twelve quiet people who sit against the big, white wall; but here comes that mean man who says bad things about me—spoiled, reckless, defiant, cruel, sociopath— no one will believe him because I am not those things—am I?

The twelve people who sat quietly and listened to people talk about me are gone now—and I wonder why some of them cried when they heard these awful stories about me—anyway, they are coming back now and none of them are looking at me and I wonder if they are embarrassed to look at me because they are ashamed to have believed those nasty lies about me.

The man in the black robe says that I have to stay for fifteen years in a faraway place with other bad people—but I never hurt anybody—why won't they listen to me?

And where is my beautiful car?

I am lonely here—my mommy sometimes visits me but my friends don't—they did once and promised to come back but they don't anymore—I guess they're too busy having the kind of fun I used to have, so I guess I really can't blame them;

gosh, it is lonely here without my foot upon the car-that-never-seemed-to-slow-down; gee, if I could just get into my car just one more time and start driving and keep driving and never stop, I'll bet that all of my problems would just disappear...

And why are all of these ugly women staring at me all the time—what do they want from me?

* * * * *

Lucy Vargas had entered the Chino Women's Correction Facility—the local folk call it prison—a sweet, ripe California peach blossoming scarlet and shocking pink, with firm, pearly white petals and a perfumed essence that swept in every available suitor in the area; and now, after suffering the degradations and perversions of the penal system—just as if they were infectious organisms that had invaded her mind and leeched out her raw talent for survival and eroded her magnificent will to live—she was a hollowed-out, worn-down, lusterless sad sack of sagging flesh and weak bones, possessing a hacked-out, burned-out look—as if something unseen and powerful had been stealing the very vibrant flush color from her very high cheekbones—as if her once-beauteous visage had been submerged in a filthy swamp and rubbed savagely in grit and grime until it absorbed all her indigenous matter—as if her once-beauteous countenance had been held too close to the hot flame that gives life to those who respect its inherent dangers. In this rock fortress she had become hooked on methamphetamines, heroin and alcohol; she smoked like a rock-red chimney in a Wyoming winter; she rarely exercised and ate the mostly burnt meat and hard biscuits, and drank cheap white wine like it was sugar water; to wit, it was as if a litter, a colony, an entire race of parasites had been introduced into her internal physiology and let loose to consume her diseased organs and glands.

But she did discover reading, and her starving mind locked onto it like a hungry dog biting into a big, juicy, white bone— but it was a mind that could never be appeased.

When she was released five years early, it was a sizzling summer day; she was met by heavy, grey smog and an absence of familiar faces; and so, like a dog once caged and now seeking its old home, she made her way back to the fertile environs where once her beauty and boldness had wrapped her up in royalty and renown.

The town was the same: fearless teenagers raced their sleek cars up and down the boulevard, looking for adventure they would never find and seeking answers they could never understand; and still there were the beach worshippers and the quaint shops, and the fresh, briny air and the sound of vitality of the ocean as it poured its mighty waves onto the pristine, white shores; and she thought that because she was home and here once had been life and joy, these revitalizing energies would befall her once again.

When the older male folk heard tell of her uncouth homecoming, and her unsettled, filthy appearance, and, in particular, the famine in her fading spirit for drugs and her easy assenting to anything as long as it resulted in a momentary body jolt, they hopped into their old sports cars and hightailed it straight to the once-precious and previously untouchable cheerleader and queen of the ball, to taste long-desired albeit rotten, forbidden meat.

The old days and their old ways could not be found by Lucy, for her life had been forged in a golden sphere spun by the ebullient fires of unrestrained youth; and now she was a bedraggled, and besmirched, cannibalized and catatonic, hooded creature who haunted the old spots and old acquaintances, only to find they were illusions that had been created when first she had stepped into the concrete-mind fortress that is prison; there was nothing here for her now because she had built nothing then, and what she had once contributed was like the house built on sand; she was aimless—that is to say, she had no good idea where to go now; she was purposeless, in that she had no real reason to be either here or there; and she was lifeless, which is to say she did not care to live and preferred to die, as she knew now that her life had been a vacuous bowl of dust and fumes and that she had never understood what life was or how one lived successfully or how one attained happiness or normalcy—but mainly because of the maddening night-mares transformed into flesh, that once boiled into a chunky soup, were poured onto her squirming brain every disturbing day and restless night—the stark vision of the dead-him, the loud bang and slam and crunch of his hard bones against the hard-yet-fragile windshield of her scarred memory.

She felt as if her body were composed of a soft wax that sloughed off and left a slime trail everywhere she walked. "There I go," she would mumble, knitting her rusty, burnt-look-ing, thick brown eyebrows as she imagined seeing her beating heart lying on the roadside; and she cared not, and cared more for ceasing to exist than existing as a phantom-carcass of her once-stunning self. "If I cannot be beautiful and loved, I want to be dead and buried; for beauty is all a woman has when she is young; it is her rite of passage through this hateful world." Yet she no longer felt young, but haggard, and dried out within, and hollow, like a dead log that had been devoured by voracious termites; therefore, she took considerable aim at disentangling her life from the living by pursuing those endeavors that posed the greatest physical risk to herself: by frequenting the middle of the road in cold embrace of eventide, by offering up her body as sacrifice to criminal spirits of the night, by imbibing copious and dangerous drugs; but she also meant to murder her mind—by allowing any and all lustful men to ravage her diseased body, by consuming more hard liquor than food; and she was well on her way to succeeding, too, when she happened upon a woman who was working at a local homeless shelter.

It was a shelter the residents had not wanted because they believed it encouraged those unworthy souls who had lost their way in the world to hang about—like importunate insects—in their fair city; but the local churches had prevailed and the shelter had stayed.

The middle-aged woman with the plain blue jeans and white blouse, this blonde-haired woman with no makeup on and a mechanical motion in pouring hot, steaming soup into the cups of the smelly recipients in line, had looked up at Lucy, she who once ruled the streets, who was now as ugly and desolate-looking as the sterile crater of a bomb blast, and stared at her briefly, then ladled soup into a white, hard plastic cup and passed it over the brown card table as she said, matter-of-factly, "You murdered my son."

Lucy stood stone still as the horror of this statement sent ripples of shock throughout her pale body; she did not move, could not move, any more than a woman frozen in ice for a thousand years could move.

The woman continued to serve up more dishes of the invigorating chicken and vegetable soup even as she said, "Please move back and let others by." Lucy obliged. The woman still was not looking up at her. "You lost ten years of your precious life," she stated, still sober of tone, "and you look like your body is rotting from the inside out," and then her voice assumed the mantle of judgment and justice as she stopped serving other wayfarers and then looked up at the accused, "but any pain you suffer is not sufficient to recompense the wanton loss of human life, nor the pain—a pain like a dead baby I carry inside me," and she clutched her breasts, "I live with every working moment and every sleeping hour," and then she dropped her flushed countenance and continued on with serving more guests in a steady, rhythmic, precise and emotionless manner.

Lucy E. Vargas was aghast; she was effectively nailed to the very hard wood upon which she teetered; she neither spoke nor gestured, but stared, with a blanched countenance, with a fixed terror, at the mechanical, smooth movements of the slender woman before her and was awed by the magnificently emotional detachment of a mother who had recently flung her umbilical cord—which served as physical bond between her only baby and herself—at Lucy, a still wet and pulsing cord that wrapped tightly around her dirty neck and squeezed it tight; and for a vivid moment, Lucy imagined what it must be like to have given birth—she herself having had six abortions, so, she reasoned, she knew at least a bit of the whole laborious business, but perhaps not for a baby suckled at a loving mother's breast, a mother who had watched the baby grow up straight and tall and true, only to see him cut down by a reckless youth, "such as you," she muttered to her incredulous self; and she wanted to offer a profound apology to the woman but found only a profound dryness in her throat that caught her sputtering words like flies in tree sap.

Still, she would sit down and heartily consume the hot soup, for hunger usurped shame now, and the infinite possibilities of "later" were always an easily accessible way out for the present.

But now Lucille, the drug addict, ex-convict, prostitute, alcoholic, criminal and all-star parasite on society, had something tangible to grasp, a mission to follow, a goal to achieve; and something once dead and incessantly begging for life clamored for acknowledgement, and coerced her to do something good as opposed to something bad, this repressed, oppressed, vilified thing in her called: conscience.

Lucy ate three bowlfuls of the life-giving hot soup and then walked outside the life-sustaining place and felt the first droplets of rain upon her disheveled and dirty, matted, blonde and stringy, brown-roots-showing hair; but she would not be dissuaded now and so took up residence under a ledge of a restaurant across the street, and patiently waited; at eleven o'clock of the p.m., a woman exited the shelter, extended her black umbrella, buttoned up her black, long overcoat, and proceeded to walk home, completely unaware that the executioner of her boy followed not too far behind.

It wasn't too long until the mother came to rest at her humble home, on the same street her precious boy had been delivered into the needlessly overflowing arms of that faithless servant, Death.

She paused at her front door. The cold rain was coming down in hard torrents when she said—and somehow her voice slit through, like sharp daggers, the harsh sheets of pounding showers—but perhaps it was not the volume of her voice but the dissonance of tone, the application of enmity and venom that prevailed against a cacophony of music supplied by mere rain. "I know what you want, and I won't give it to you." Her back was still to the lone figure who stood in the empty street. "Go away, go away and crawl into a deep hole." She inserted her key into the lock and waited for further instructions from the shifting winds that are Fate.

"I am dead," Lucille said, her sorrowful voice surfing back on the waiting, discordant wave of her accuser.

"Good." Yet, the key still lay unmoved in the cold steel lock.

"Even if I kill myself, it doesn't bring back your boy."

"You're right—there is nothing you can say or do; nothing," she murmured, and then her head fell back and a frightening species of glee landed upon her visage, "but O, how I dearly wish you would…"

A car was coming down the road at an extremely high rate of speed.

"If I suffered every day for eternity, you would rather have your boy."

Her voice was plastered by a frustrated want. "You can go to Hell and I will still have my boy."

"Life cannot be this unfair—it just cannot."

The car full of screaming teenagers was fast approaching.

She nearly smiled, but it changed to irony and thus irony smiled. "Oh, yes, it is—it is when you're a reckless, low-life, arrogant little tramp who doesn't care about anyone but herself."

"I care about you now."

Now, the mother, who would grieve for her dead son forever, turned abruptly, her face aflame with righteous indignation. "Oh, criminals are always so sorry for the victim's relatives after it's all over—but what good is that?" She threw up her hands in a wild gesture, dropping her umbrella. "Why are you alive—why? At least have the common courtesy to go die and leave our community alone."

"Is there no going back once you trespass upon the lives of innocent people?"

"No!"

The speeding car with the drunken youths was nearly upon Lucille, and the woman instinctively yelled for her to move, which Lucille refused to do, but merely cast an uninterested gaze upon the speeding vehicle, which presently splashed close by her and then raced on, its drug-smashed occupants never cognizant of the human being standing in the road.

"You are crazy," the woman said, shaking her head slowly.

"You can't kill that which is already dead."

The mother displayed a hard countenance that was born from thinking of her dead child every waking moment and in dreaming of him in every haunted dream, and spoke in a tone that was fashioned from the hatred she carried inside her. "I only wish I could."

"Is there no forgiveness for our imperfections, which in error we magnify?"

"No." It was a solitary, mean, monolithic pronouncement carved from rancor and rebuke.

"Is there nothing I can do to atone for my sins? No good deeds, no selfless acts?"

"No."

Lucille stood, defeated at every philosophical and emotional and spiritual summit, a prisoner of a single, solitary ill-circumstance. "And what of your son, had he life for a moment before us, would he, too, so easily and eagerly condemn me?"

Ah, but now the woman hesitated in her swift rebuttal, and disagreeable reply, and outraged outburst, and settled into a mild melancholy.

Lucille may have been a degenerate lump of diseased and dying flesh, but she was still a woman and could sense the ritualistic rites the mother practiced while loathing her at the temple of grief, tumble, and fall into ruin.

"My boy," the mother returned, her rough tone softened now, her hard voice assuaged by the perfumed lubricant of blessed memories, and then she slowly walked out into the pouring rain and stood in front of Lucille; her voice yielded humanness now, tenderness now, and joy. "My boy would have never allowed anyone to hurt him without forgiving him." She smiled in fond remembrance. "When he was six years old, the neighborhood bully pushed him down and kicked him and hit him, and my boy said to him, 'It's okay, it's not your fault you're unhappy, and if you need a friend, I'll be there for you'." She nearly wept. "The two boys became best friends—the boy was even a pallbearer..." She shook her head. "That is why I don't understand why you came back here—surely he forgave you."

Lucille frowned as she knit her eyebrows and stared hard at the woman. "No, I don't know that at all—no—I pray that I did know."

"Tommy would never hurt a living creature," the woman began again, as if this was her child's epitaph, "he would never even hurt a dead one—he hated even to pull out weeds." She smiled briefly, but it was consumed in the conflagration that is sorrow. "He would carefully pull out those cute yellow dandelions from the front yard and lay them carefully on the ground, apologizing to them—and then take them to a field and replant them—and O, how they would grow!" She nodded her head in agreement, as if she needed to acknowledge that she still remembered this and must never forget it. "So, I say to you, Tommy would never let a human being leave if he thought that person would be sad because of him—no, never, not my Tommy—you see," she whispered, as if saying it for the first time with devotion and affection, "he was a special person, and this world did not deserve so kind and gentle a soul such as he." But then her civility was plowed under by enmity, and she said in a guttural whisper, "And to think he was killed by a sociopath like you," and she turned and walked away, and this time she turned the key in the lock and went inside and shut the door.

Lucille turned and spied the very spot that so long ago had undone her so completely; or, as she now thought, simply revealed who she had always been, but which had been so skillfully disguised by artifice and illusion.

She stood on the muddy dirt path next to the road and gazed at the multicolored glasses and pictures and brightly colored plastic flowers that still stood in the exact spot the man had fallen, and she knelt to her knees in front of this and then lay down so that she faced this beautiful homage.

Thus, her vigil in the small pools and brown mud began, and here she would stay, unmolested by passersby, who reasoned, as they beheld her curled-up, slender form, that for them, being dry and getting to where they wanted to be had more merit than getting involved with a common vagrant; she would lie here now, she decided, until she could gain knowledge about the man she had killed that terrible day and how it might bring some chance at tranquility inside her tumultuous mind. She closed her eyes and listened.

Water is the oldest language of the world—it carries the ancient script of creation, it contains the sacred codex of Man's history, it speaks in the esoteric language of Nature—it carves out the deepest canyons and fills up the tiniest holes; it cannot be destroyed, it is never destroyed—it is in everything and writes our future with every precious molecule; and rain is its messenger, its Mercury, its bringer of joy and destruction; yet in it there resides its own dialect that whispers secrets and revelations to anyone who knows how to keep their mind and heart clear of the interference and clamor of useless and needless noise.

Lucille heard the pain of her failed past beg for mercy, and she unhooked its sharp talons, which had dug deep into her fragile psyche, and released them into the abyss of curses; this took some time, but when it was completed she was free of a heretical faith that had punctured her heart and bled her dry while she worshipped at its fleshly altar; she heard now the gentle, steady, pounding of the rain droplets; she heard their musical song and listened as her mind absorbed the rhythmic pattern of earth's tears as they landed upon liquid, dirt and asphalt; her mind began to unwind the seemingly meaningless noise and then dissect it: first she heard the subtle piercing of rain into puddles, and she heard a harmony therein; she heard the cold rain smash into the soft dirt, and she heard a lyrical note therein; she heard the rain pound the asphalt, and she heard a hard voice of song, therein; and so when she allowed her mind to revel in all three nocturnes, this blend of music and chorus became distinct to her, and the first act of this opus opened her mind to the very day she sought to see.

The assembling of the stark image of the man being delivered unto death came quickly, as it was an image in her mind's eye as much as the icy black sky or the sparkling blue sea or the twinkling white stars; she heard the pitter-patter of the tiny raindrops as she looked deeper into this widening vision; the heart of this choral symphony danced and caressed her mind as she slowed down the commotion of the images; the hot sun of that very day she felt now against her face and the music of the spheres cradled her and stroked her as she saw the face of the man; she saw him standing now in front of her rampaging car, a picture she had never beheld before: his handsome youth, his kind face, and his posture was relaxed and his face quiet of fear and rage; and he said to her, as plainly as if he had been standing next to her that accursed day—and she saw his mouth move and plainly speak with undeniable compassion:

"I forgive you."

He had said it, she knew now, he had said it even when imminent death was unfurled before him. "Forgive me," she said to him, as she saw him still standing there; and then he smiled, and behold, he held out his slender hands, and she held out her hands, too, and he grasped them and gently pulled her through the now-porous barrier of the car; and as they stood together, adorned in a shower of shimmering white light, they watched the car dissolve and melt away into the too-often-forgotten and often-neglected sea of forgetfulness; and lo, he crowned her soul in ephemeral glory, and his soul grew even greater in glory because of it.

Her pious tears adorned her face as they trickled down to the liquid rivers below; and these were true tears of penitence, joined in the searching dialogue of Mankind that spoke of the eternal struggle to be human, and live free of the bondage of sin and temptation and of the self-righteousness and arrogance of self.

She died, then; yet, somehow, in those last moments alive, as her neglected body lay huddled up alongside the soaked road, she had truly understood that she belonged to a sisterhood of beings who cannot and will not live apart from each other and must continually join in the battle to live in peace—despite their smallest and widest differences—with each other, and the world.

-Finis-

March of Life

The prisoners were marching along as if they could be felled by the tiniest puff of wind against their fragile bodies or the smallest increase of heat across their burning skin; they were weary and exhausted, their minds were fraying and their resistance to the prodding of their antagonist was ebbing.

They had been captured long ago after fighting continuously for many days and they were already malnourished and sick, and long ago the march to the camp of the enemy had begun; the war was raging on but they had their own war on now, and this was one that had been clearly delineated by their captors, to wit: to fall or fall behind meant death, to stop without permission meant death, to harangue their captors or look upon them without the proper countenance of submission meant death, to whine or complain or evince any emotion other than utter complacency meant death or physical agony; so, this was the peripheral war of the prisoners now, their private war, and the other war might as well have been on the moon.

This was a smaller war now inside the bigger war, yet still a war of no little consequence, and still fought with the same aggression as the other war, but with different tactics: not with bullets, but verbiage; not with physical muscle, but muscular emotion; not for overt victory, but the victory of mere survival—and it was a war of physical strength and physical endurance and mental will to withstand that which the body had never experienced nor should ever experience and, once experienced, must never experience again. Yet it was now, and now could not be abrogated, and so this living funeral procession dragged on, leaving a very long line of the very battered and mangled bodies of courageous men who had fought and fought with great valor in battle after battle over many months and sometimes years in the big and important war, but many of whom were now fated to die in the bloody mouth of this cunning serpent whose morals slumbered in the smoking graves of every nation its pernicious breath breathed upon.

The time was high noon and the air was humid and sizzling and the prisoners were thirsty and pouring out great amounts of precious sweat onto their scorched skin; they had not been fed in too many hours and in too many hours more they had not tasted the sweet elixir that is the soft, silky, universal liquid that soothes the parched tongue and quenches the dire thirst and brings life to the dehydrated body the world over; and still, the prisoners marched on, affixing their mental horizon on one small task, and that was to not physically or emotionally fail.

At the beginning of this long march, the prisoners had not quite understood the significance of being punished for following the logical dictates of their waning strength, to wit: seeking rest after being coerced to walk for a prolonged distance in savage conditions with little food or drink; they had not comprehended the absolute intolerance of their captors toward a man wanting a much-deserved respite, but soon they were wise to the repercussions of a prisoner seeking the solace of soil and shade based on his own self-interest, and so the message went down the line that to touch the ground with knee or hand or to lag behind meant a hasty cessation of life.

The captors were not very clever in their punishment of their captives; no, indeed, not nearly as clever as their European counterparts, who were restless masters and well practiced in the art of highly imaginative and well-groomed torture against their prisoner of war.

"Hey, Joe," a youthful soldier with a brown beard whispered in a voice drained of energy, "I feel like I can't go on."

"You can make it, Rusty," the older man with the steel, light green helmet on his round, balding head replied, "you're young and strong."

"But I can't, Sergeant, I just don't feel..." But then his hoarse voice seemed to cramp and seize up and lie there, as if his words were marooned in a barren desert and split open so that their guts were dried out; but then in a little while, as if a gently falling dew had landed upon his swelling tongue, he said, "Tell Betsy I love her, huh, would ya, Sarge..."

Sergeant Joseph Cappinelli looked back and expected to see the youth still bent over but still walking, still evincing a mask of pain but struggling on, but he was astonished to see the man sitting in the shade of a palm tree. "No," he shouted, unable to suppress his shock. He received a harsh pounding on his head from the brown, wooden rifle butt of one of his guards, but he did not feel the blow as he watched the small soldier come up to the boy and in one continuous motion raise his rifle and shoot him dead and then reach down and wrench his silver dog tags away and then turn and walk past the sergeant and in one more continuous motion smack him in the face with his rifle butt; and then the sneering guard hesitated for a moment to see if the man would fall from the blow, and when he realized he would not, he moved on down the line, issuing admonitions to any prisoner who looked back at the dead soldier.

"Break!" the same guard yelled several seconds later, and watching the happy faces of the prisoners as they began to head their weary bodies toward the cool shade of the palm trees, he did smile. "Right where you are, you imperialist dogs!" And as the men began to bend their weary bodies toward the hot ground, he yelled out, "Stand, you dogs!" He smiled largely when the prisoners displayed visages of displeasure, and so he ordered his men to beat those soldiers who had done thus. "Stand!" he said, smiling, walking past the prisoners, "and enjoy the sun," and he moved toward his men, who were giving out canteens that were filled with cool water from nearby artesian wells and white rice balls wrapped in white cloth to their brethren; he looked over to the prisoners and nodded and sniffed and playfully nudged another officer and then muttered something to him as he pointed toward the prisoners; the other officer, munching on his sweet rice, nodded his head as he looked over at the men who were baking in the hot sun like captured game.

On the side of the road there was a dirty, filthy, maggot-ridden buffalo wallow that the officer had also pointed out to his friend while he had that mischievous twinkle in his brown eyes; occasionally he and the other officer would glance over at the wavering prisoners, gesturing to them while they were eating and drinking and sitting under the cool shade of the high palm trees; occasional shots would ring out, and subordinates would come up from behind, their black rifle barrels still hot or their bayonets bloody from the job they had just done. One of them told the commanding officer that there were no more dying prisoners, and he handed him the mess of dog tags, which the officer then deposited onto the ground just as if he were ridding his hands of filthy waste.

And then it happened: one of the prisoners broke and ran to the buffalo wallow and began to drink the dirty water, his greedy slurping sounds ricocheting throughout the temporary camp; several of the other prisoners, seeing no ill thing happening to their comrade, and staring in astonishment at this sight, began to move forward, too.

"No," Joe declared, but he knew that the men, many of whom had come from different divisions, would not heed his advice, and so he watched helplessly as four men rushed to the small stream of disease-infested water.

The captor-officer in charge smiled and nodded his small, round head as he looked at this scene and then looked to the other officer, who presently gave him his tasty rice ball; the officer in charge smiled and then shouted out to several of his men an explicit order, which the men immediately executed.

The five soldiers who were lying on their aching stomachs at least died with the taste of liquid nourishment in their dry mouths.

"Sergeant," one of the men murmured as he stared in horror at the macabre sight, "I don't think they would have cared if they knew they were going to die." He looked around with great circumspection and then whispered, "My people have been watching us—they will try and get us food."

Joe watched as the soldiers took the dog tags off the dead men. "Your people need to be as careful as we are, for these soldiers will kill anyone who tries to help us."

The man smiled in fond reflection and then whispered, "The Filipino people are grateful for what the Allies have done and will risk their lives to bring comfort to us."

Joe reflected upon this for a moment and then whispered, "It is enough that so many of us will die for a bigger cause, but also to appease the iniquitous soul of these beasts incarnate; and yet it is our duty to harass and defy the enemy even as we suffer under the yoke of his tyranny." He looked upon the five dead men and he remembered what he was and what he had become these last years of furious fighting, and he felt pride swell in his breast. "And by this, I mean that we might try and escape and die as men and not as slaves." He looked around at the men who were shielding the intense sun with their brown fingers and desperate to keep their balance. "Who will go with me?"

The men around him did not know him and therefore would not throw their lot in with him; but the Filipino man with the small growth of black beard, who had spoken to him on several occasions, had developed a bit of trust in him and so said, "I will go with you; it is better to die as a soldier than in the yoke of tyranny."

One of the captor-soldiers walked up to the two men and said with a scowl, "Empty your pockets." The two men did so, and the Filipino soldier produced a small trinket that he had found on the battlefield a week ago. The soldier shot him through the head right there and then, and then said, in a calm and steady voice as he held up the small, silver, Japanese ornament, "Any prisoner who is found with items taken from Japanese soldiers they have killed…" And then he looked at the sergeant and turned his pistol on him and shot him too through the head. "Any prisoner who is even seen talking to a prisoner who took an item after killing an honorable Japanese soldier…" And he walked away with a proud and strong strut that signified to his fellows that indeed he was a strong and uncompromising soldier who did not dither nor dawdle in his dealings with these prisoners he considered subhuman, animalistic barbarians.

The line moved on after this forever hour of brutal scorching in the broiling sun, and as they struggled on, the prisoners were witness to other men who had died near the buffalo wallows and other men who had died after falling behind and other men who had fallen down and were bayoneted or shot and later crushed by trucks and Jeeps as they lay either dead or dying; there were prisoners who had been beheaded by officers on horseback who were using samurai swords and who subsequently spat on the corpses as a sign that they evinced no respect for men who surrendered during combat; there were dead men near the artesian wells, and dead Filipino women who had been raped and then physically mutilated by their we-are-superior-to-the-world-and-we-will-show-you-by-our-actions captors; there were dead Filipino men and women and even little girls and boys who had attempted to secretly throw food to the valiant Allied soldiers who had sought to liberate them from their conquerors; there was death everywhere, stinking, rotting, foul death sitting idle in the breezeless air and the prisoners were walking in it and falling in it and smelling it and it filled their senses and invaded their minds and eroded their will to live and live sanely, if even for the briefest of time.

This was only one small group of many small groups who were part of a larger contingent of many other groups as they marched on their long journey toward the sweltering metallic-coffins-disguised-as-railroad-cars that would transport them to a particular place where they would then be forced to walk even more miles until they reached the enemy camp where disease would continue to slay them and where their fresh corpses would then be planted like smelly refuse in deepening graves.

Near the end of this long human train of misery and torture were small, straggling groups of captors and prisoners, and the job of many of the guards here was to ensure that the men who had already fallen were dead and that their dog tags were ripped from them. The prisoners in these walking deliriums had the opportunity to see all the mistakes their forward-walking comrades had made, and so they were in a unique position to gain wisdom from this and perhaps their lives; and it was in this way that the men who were murdered at the front of the long march did not die in vain but might have given life to those who marched behind them.

There was a man who was marching in this late hour not with a visage of wrath poking holes in the heavy heat that swirled like irksome flies about him, but with a face of good humor and glad tidings; he had been thus since the journey began and even despite the fearful spirit that had descended upon the staggering men, that beat them down into heaps of bruised flesh and broken bone. He had been kind and generous to every man about him—carrying litters for the wounded until his captors decided the wounded needed to die; helping one man after another hobble along and imparting courage and hope to them until his captors decided that they too needed to die. If Man hath a soul, one of his comrades said of him, then he hath one, and the noblest.

"Frank," said another soldier to him as they walked along a dirt road that was strewn with the ripped-apart and mutilated, stinking, rotting corpses of Allied soldiers and indigenous people, "given a hammer, would you not beat your captors to a painful and slow death?" But he had spoken thus with sharp words dipped in the thick blood of his hated enemies.

Frank—his eyes of blue, blue as cornflowers, blue as a bright spring sky—gave forth a barely imperceptible shake of his blonde head, and looked westward, and then said in a gentle voice that bore malice toward none, "Where the rosy-covered dawn breaks, my love calls to me."

The other man frowned and nearly stumbled but Frank effortlessly caught him up in arms that seemed too small to exert such strength. "But what about these lousy…"

Frank merely looked again toward the melting of pale light into the dark embers of encroaching night and then said in a blissful tone, "She who is more to me than the fortunes of the world awaits me; and she calls me, thus," and he slowed his walk and bent his head as if to listen to a honey-scented voice that only he could hear. "I must seek her; for even now, she needs me."

"What, eh, Frank? What do you say?"

Frank had nearly stopped now and was still looking with great wonder to the western-leaning skies when he declared in a solemn tone, "I must go to her," and he began to turn around and walk, in earnest, toward this place his mind had built for him out of faith and devotion, but his comrade halted him.

"Frank, the guards!"

One of the soldiers came running up to the two men, bearing his weapon in dire threat toward them, and shouting so that the other guards might hear the merciless chord of violence in his soaring voice, "Go back, you dogs!"

Frank was smiling still and still peering into the soul of Peace and Joy, and he said, his voice cradled in wonderment and his heart bathed in the blessed aura of Love, "She needs me now, and so I must leave, now."

"You cannot go," the guard said, defiantly, and then said in a guttural and low whisper, "If you do, I must shoot you."

Frank saw the guard now for the first time, and poured a gaze of purity upon the youth, and he nodded, "While I am who I am, now, I suddenly can see; as I stand here, now, and gaze upon you, I can see you as you are," his head rose up and he looked over the slender youth and then cast his intense look into his brown eyes, "and you carry the sword in displeasure; it crowns you with a crown of thorns and creates the scepter of wickedness you must carry, and you weep for what you must do, and for what you cannot do."

The guard evinced incredulity and his face was full of wrath. "You must stay in the line or you will be shot!"

Frank merely smiled. "You cannot harm that which cannot be harmed; you cannot do what must not be done; you can only do what is to be done, and what is to be done is not your will."

"Get back in line, you filthy imperialist!"

Frank smiled once more as he tilted his head and beheld the consternation of the youth. "I find no enmity in you toward your fellow man; you should not be here."

"What!" the youth cried, his face aglow with wrath. "Not be a proud Japanese soldier! We, who will rule the world! We, who will conquer every nation before us!"

Frank shook his head. "But not you."

The youth nearly swung his rifle butt at the bold American soldier but relented, and his breath was quick and his emotions were hot when he stood up and proudly sang out, "You are defiant; you should be shot! Don't you know that our armies are like mountains descending upon hills, like oceans swallowing up rivers—we are as the stars in the heaven shining the light of Japan upon a cowering world!"

And then Frank said, in a voice that frightened the youth, for it had no rancor in it, no malice, no vengeance, but the seed of tranquility and serenity and forgiveness, "And yet Love will turn your mountains to wax, and boil away your oceans, and cause your stars to fall from the sky," and he looked again toward the beckoning west, and his voice became even softer, "Do you know that my love calls me, my love, whom I have always known, whom I will never be without, calls to me, even now; and I will be with her, even now, and nothing earthly may change that."

The wife of Frank Petrocelli was at that precise moment in the hospital room of the maternity ward, back in her small town in the States.

The soldier pressed his lips together and his chest was heaving, and then he said, "I will shoot you if you try and escape!"

"What you will do, you must do; but what you do, you cannot do to me unless it has been appointed since time immemorial; and so I tell you once more, I will go now to be with she who needs me." And he turned to leave, but the soldier barred his way. "I will be with she who is more important to me than my own life and the life of this world; and what you do cannot stop me," and he put his hand upon the bony shoulder of the soldier, "what you do now will give life to yourself, too; so it has been written at the beginning of time."

At that moment, the wife of Frank Petrocelli was giving birth to a baby boy.

"You cannot go," the soldier said, his voice impaled now by doubt and suffused with diffidence, "I have orders to shoot deserters." Regret stabbed wounds into the animated face of the young man.

"I will go now," Frank said, calmly, nodding again and smiling again, "and what you do, do now, and you will give life to me and to yourself," and he turned to go once more and walked around the soldier and his bewildered comrades.

"Stop!" the Japanese soldier shouted, looking around now and sweating like one in anguish and fear, "please stop," he said in a lower voice, and in a still-lower voice filled with that villain, uncertainty, "or I must shoot, I must, you see, it is orders…"

With every step he made toward the country of his beloved, he could feel the blessed union with her transforming in front of him. The Japanese guard was looking around and trembling and looking around and seeing the other American prisoners trembling and he was still looking around and seeing no other guards and he was still trembling when he looked again to Frank, who was slowly moving out of sight; and then he looked up the road and saw another guard looking suspiciously his way, and then it just happened: he shot; and then something else just happened—he was running toward Frank and warm tears were streaming down his ruddy face and he was not ashamed as he came upon the struggling man while imploring in a hoarse whisper, "O, it is all a tragic mistake, don't you see—we did not have the resources for so many prisoners, so none of this should have happened…but you must forgive me, forgive me, I have never killed before…"

Frank looked up at the youth and reached out his hand to touch his flushed face. "Nor have you killed now."

At that exact moment, the wife and newborn baby boy of Frank Petrocelli died.

Frank looked up into the dark canopy of the starry sky and smiled. "And now we are three; and you have given life to me this very day, for this very day I shall be in paradise with my family; and this very day, you shall be free from the prison you walk in." And he, too, died.

The other guards came running up to the youth and when they found him weeping, berated him for his disgraceful conduct, and then one of them ripped the silver dog tags off the dead-prisoner-but-now-set-free-American and threw them at the youth and then walked back to the lines.

This last line of prisoners hung their heads low and wiped away a pious tear and then moved on.

* * * * *

Genji knew that his life was over. He had committed an unforgivable sin against the great towering sphinx that was the Red Rising Sun—he had evinced weakness in the carrying out of executing a prisoner; but he had always known that this day was coming, for he had never wanted to do what his peers had done, to wit: to kill with a zealous pride and rape with glee and boasting, and slaughter without conscience innocent citizens and slaughter without cause innocent prisoners and commit any act the great red, flowing flag had promised they might do with impunity—as they were now the conquerors of the world, and as conquerors, just like those past, could do as they pleased, as was their right since time immemorial; but Genji Haki had never believed any of it and even prayed to escape this war that burrowed into his skull like a loud and propagating tic; he was not a proud warrior but a shamed weakling who dreamed of painting and reading books and family life. He hated his fellow soldiers and he hated Japan. "How did he know who I was," he wondered about the prisoner he had killed, as he walked behind his company of soldiers, wondering if they had spread the word of his great misdeeds. He was soon to find out that they had not.

The expert blackmailer is truly an artisan; he is neither timid nor afraid, but gifted in the ways of persuasion; he is crafty like the snake, ferocious like the bear, cunning like the fox; he is arrogant as a king, and dedicated like a sculptor who carves out each segment of his statue according to the dictates of his imagination; so it was with the men who had witnessed the grave misdeed of Genji and now walked with him, as they began to molest his peace of mind and demand every kind of favor from him; and thus, they meant to pilfer and rob him of his dignity and pride and solitude until they had squeezed him and left him to rot in the sun like the corpse of a dead animal; and although he was only twenty-two years of age, he knew what was to come, as he was educated beyond the abilities of his tormentors; and so, he maneuvered his commander into assigning him a position he had previously held and then he headed for the coast.

The intelligent man, be he physically weak or strong, has an advantage over his common counterpart-foe, and it is this: no matter what the common man-foe does, or says, or practices or promises, or provokes, or threatens, or seeks to destroy, or rages against, or sets his mind to, the intelligent man can outwit him and get around him and outmaneuver him and the poor common fool will never know what has transpired; and while it is true that the intelligent man may never get the most beautiful woman or the greatest riches or have the most power, he will survive, he will find his niche, he will last long past the early and ignominious deaths of his persecutors because he knows how to live and where he should live to achieve complete serenity and harmony.

Genji, until this dark day, had thus far avoided the awful trappings of war, the terrible bloodshed, the sickening triumph of bludgeoning dead bodies and raping of foreign women and torturing of Allied prisoners by constantly maneuvering to be in positions where he would be in between the battle; a messenger, if you will, between the fighting, a traveler who neither partook in nor reveled in any victory nor lamented any defeat, a soldier existing solely on the outside of his brothers-in-arms who sought and begged and happily engaged in any campaign to exterminate Allied troops or humiliate any Allied prisoner or degrade and murder any conquered citizen; he was the messenger between outfits, the runner between units and squadrons, the man freely moving around and outside the fighting but still seen as a valuable entity who courageously delivered important information and was viewed as an essential part of winning the war against the entire free world; thus, he would play this role again, having acquired a well-rounded knowledge of how to approach officers in battalions and what to say to them and how to act toward them and the proper way to extract information out of them that would lead him to the next safe haven through this nightmarish but, more importantly, untamed and spreading apocalypse.

He knew the names of virtually every officer on this island and he could retrieve those names from his extraordinary memory, and he also had knowledge of every major battle here and its results and he had memorized all the maps and coordinates he had carried, and so he could insert this information into whatever plotting scenario he needed to gently nudge a commander to say what he wanted him to say, so Genji might continue on toward the coast that held the sailing vessels to take him away from this grief and despair; it is true that he had been coerced into joining his former regiment because there was a lack of soldiers, but he would not allow this to happen again.

The first time he met a commander of a unit, the man was exhausted and expecting good news from the east, and Genji was certain to impart such a communiqué to him; the commander rewarded Genji with warm praise and offered him food and drink and then sent him on his way to the next unit; it was in this way that the slender young man with the head of thick, black hair and silver-rimmed glasses weaved

his way through the jungle, by stitch: handing over information an officer longed to hear; by loop: by directing the officer
through the information given to move Genji further across
the jungle chessboard; by strand: by building a complicated
story that was begun by the last officer and strengthened by
the next one; and soon, after traversing the dense jungle and
seeing more prisoner-of-war lines and more bloated corpses
of citizens and more bloody battlefields that were strewn with
the bodies of many soldiers from both sides, he was at the
blessed sea and he was boarding a naval ship with a legal doc-
ument that gave him free passage back to Japan and a note of
commendation that spoke of his bravery and intelligence in
relaying information through enemy lines for many months. He
went to sleep that peaceful night as if he had just been named
Emperor and awoke during the clamorous morning to find
out that he was in a sinking sepulcher; he jumped overboard
wearing the red safety vest he had had the foresight to secure
when first he boarded the ship, and after he had floated for a
day in the cold waters of the Atlantic Ocean, he was washed
ashore and upon awakening the next morning was greeted
with four rifles aimed at him and a flurry of words in a language that throttled him from his superior brain down to his
small, calloused feet. "Get up," the men yelled in Chinese.

* * * * *

He was their prisoner now, on the last geographical point
in the world he would have picked; he was bound and gagged
and placed upside down on a wooden pole and carried just like
a lion that has been stalking a village and eating the villagers
for many months and upon his capture must not be simply

put to death quickly but groomed to be expertly tortured and maimed with the most heinous cruelty imaginable.

He spoke Chinese fluently, but for now he would merely listen and learn, just as the crafty fox that is caught by the feisty hens understands their language but will bide his time as he plots a way to escape—not that Genji needed to comprehend the exact meaning of their words to divine the rancor and wrath elevated in their biting words; when he breached the periphery of the small village—every village has such a small area that, once it has been breached by an outsider, seems like a foreign and unsafe land—he could hear the tremendous commotion of the people as they came running toward him with whipping sticks and large rocks and whipping words and hurling promises of excruciating pain for him; and even as he closed his eyes and felt the commencement of beatings upon his slender frame, he tried to wade through the emotional tumult of the words that now heaped upon him like crushing stones.

"Monster, die…villain…rapist, die, die…murderer… inhuman murderer…beast…die, die, die…inhuman-murderer-rapist-foul-beast-monster die, die, die, die…" This was what he heard and no less than this and not dressed in any lighter shade of animosity or vitriolic casing, but plenty more than this and much harsher than this did the hysterical and weeping people shout and scream the closer he got to the scene of the grisly crimes freely committed against their innocent family and friends and relatives by his genetic brethren; so yes, he was the rabid black bear with the yellow fangs that had eaten the villagers, caught; he was the voracious and mad wolf that had stolen their infants and fed them to her cubs, ensnared; indeed, he was every malevolent creature from every insidious nightmare come to life and now come to be punished for the moral infractions of every Japanese soldier before him and after him; and he was to be their human sacrifice for every wrong done to them and they would not gain pleasure from it but a sense of at least one small victory for a people that had done nothing at all to suffer such unfettered torture and complete and enthusiastic annihilation from an entire invading civilization; they were clean as virgin-white, freshly powdered snow as they stood on high and judged him, and he was as guilty as the tarry-black blood dripping from the black-as-oil gaping mouth of a ghoulish phantom that devours newborn babies, and their dead loved ones would be avenged.

A donkey is surely an animal, but if you wrong him he suddenly assumes the posture of his civilized master, Homo sapiens, to wit: against a vanquished enemy that hath impugned his character, he will bend down and squat and produce copious amounts of feces upon his dead foe; yet it is the same with finely cultured and respectable Man when he feels slighted, he feels the sudden urge to expel his inner wastes upon those whom he scorns—and so in this way he becomes like the donkey; or is it that the donkey becomes like him?

As it was, the women whacked him senseless with skinny sticks and the men smacked his body over with stout ones; and the women, with positively no shame and absolutely no hesitation at all, lifted up their skirts and urinated upon the now-prostrate form of the villain, while the men dropped their pants and did the same; yet, this was only the beginning of the as-yet-uncoordinated-but-merely-spontaneous attacks, and the day was young and the people strong in body and their desire to punish, a blossoming creature gaining strength with every moment.

Genji became a human latrine and depository for every kind of rubble and filth and scum the villagers could heap and throw and pour upon him; he lay there in his ripped and torn tan uniform, covered in wounds that were bloody and numerous and soon to fester, and he with a mind that was weak and spinning into a dark abyss where he would find no refuge but only an uncomforting death. He was presently placed in a bamboo cage and left to simmer in his misery during the warm night; every noise he heard, he reckoned it was for him—being a prisoner of war in a hostile camp that seeks to flail you very slowly and with a dull, rusty blade tends to make one self-absorbed; if there was a sudden ruckus, he flinched; if there was a scream and holler, he reasoned the violent words had origins in his presence; if there were footsteps coming toward his cage—and although now he could not see who it was because his eyes were swollen shut—he knew the maker of the footsteps was coming on account of him; and as it was, he was generally correct on all accounts, and so he got continuous and vicious beatings that alternated between intensity in brevity and just plain old nasty punches and kicks and pokes and jabs that kept him awake and anxious; but what was most intriguing to him—if analysis of their actions at that moment was possible in his distressed mind—was that his tormentors now neither spoke nor cried out when they assaulted him, but executed their labor upon him with vigorous huffing and puffing, whereupon his mind then translated this into an eerie hallucination of human masks frozen in horrible grimaces that would not relent until the animosity that had frozen within them leaked out and liberated their souls from torment.

He would sleep intermittently, but intermittently the assaults would continue, thus drawing a heavy curtain of exhaustion over his consumed body; and by the coming of a blood-red dawn, he was slain in spirit and mind and wanting to die. He had a high fever now and now he was babbling about his misbegotten life as he lay curled up like a beaten kitten on the cold ground.

When sunbeams of light diffused across his swollen back in the early morning, he awoke and beheld an eerie sight: all the people of the village sitting around his cage in utter silence and staring at him in aroused curiosity; he was startled and rose up and smacked his head against the top of the thick, green bamboo and then instinctively pushed back with his feet across the dirt into a corner and held his bound hands against his thumping chest; the fever had broken but now he had the fever of fear and dread.

The elder of the village, a man dressed in simple peasant cotton clothes and wearing a white beard and whose face had no disdain at all, said rather matter-of-factly, "You have slept for two days."

He was the captured black wolf with the blazing red eyes and sharp claws who had eaten the sheep of the flock and now the sheepherder was supplying a pleasant and soothing voice to him; his eyes were darting about as his mind sought to make sense of this phantasmagoria; he was breathing so quickly and his mind racing so fast that he could not speak but merely gesticulated about at the sitting populace.

"Ah, yes," replied the old man with the sparse white hair, "they wish to hear your story." The old man moved forward a bit and spoke again, but this time in a kind and gentle voice. "You do understand me."

Yes, Genji did understand him, and then it occurred to him that the man was speaking Chinese and that the man knew that Genji understood it. "I must have spoken in Chinese while I was feverish," he decided, and then looking about, said in their native tongue, "Why have you not killed me?"

The man with the small white beard smiled. "There is an old proverb: 'when the body is sick, the mind is free to tell the truth.' Young man, you said many things about yourself and the war when you were ill." Genji sat silent. "Tell us again, Genji, and if you speak the truth, you will be set free."

Genji reflected upon this and decided that if it were a ruse, he was dead, and if it were genuine, then he had nothing to lose, and so he easily assented and narrated all that had happened on the small island he had escaped from. "And then I awoke here," he finished, "and here I am, your prisoner, so do with me what you will, and do it quickly," and he shut his eyes and bowed his head so deeply that it touched the cold ground.

The old man rose and walked over to the cage and put a key in the lock and undid the bamboo door and led Genji out. "A lie, once told, cannot be told twice," he whispered, and then he and the rest of the village knelt down in profound contrition and bowed toward Genji and asked for his forgiveness. Genji wept.

* * * * *

Genji, sitting in the small, brown hut, listened to the village elder as the young woman beside him tended his wounds; when the old man finished his narrative, Genji said, without hesitation, "I would have killed me—I would kill me now, if I were you, for you cannot trust any Japanese man or woman now, as we are all infected with the same malignant spirit; we are like a spreading plague, and the only way to stop it is to cleanse it with fire from head to foot."

The elder gazed at the young soldier and nodded his head. "And this is why you live, Genji, for you are a citizen of the world—you have transgressed beyond what defines you; Japan does not define you alone—you understand that what they do is wrong and so you embrace what is right."

"But," he protested vehemently, "my brethren have committed unspeakable acts against—"

"No," the elder said, interrupting him, "you must never say such acts are unspeakable, for then they will be forgotten, or denied in history books—this is what the past has taught us."

He screwed up his eyes and nodded when he said with great assurance, "You are an educated man."

The elder smiled. "I was a university professor of history before the Japanese army invaded."

Genji sat silent for a moment. "I apologize once more."

The old man held up his hand. "Do not apologize for the crime of others; all men are perfectly capable of committing their own crimes—and if the world had only to worry about men, and not nations, we would still have too many problems to face."

The countenance of Genji belied the philosophy of his host. "How can you forgive men such as I, who should have killed themselves rather than take an innocent life; who should have killed themselves rather than join the Japanese army; who, if I had the courage, should fight my own brethren and die a man—but I am a coward, a coward who knows what has happened in Asia, what my own people have done right here in China, what our armies have done to your villages—how they have slaughtered men and women and babies, and raped women and tortured them and dishonored men and women and killed without pity or mercy," his voice grew despondent and his face became grave, "how could such a noble people as mine do such an ignoble thing?" And he let his head fall into his hands as he sobbed, "I am ashamed to be Japanese, I would rather have the eyes of those oppressed and die with them than be a free Japanese man…"

The elder put his hand on the slim shoulders of the youth, and said in a gentle voice, "You are an old soul, a citizen of the world, who understands that there are times when even an entire nation can err."

Genji lifted up his head. "Err," he cried out, incredulous, "the Japanese army practices genocide here—it is Japan that needs a cleansing; yes, it is Japan that needs to be cleansed if the people too harbor such thoughts."

The old man shook his head. "You do not understand war, Genji, you must understand the past—the wars that have been fought in one generation between two nations are quickly forgotten and forgiven by the next one; in a generation, this war too will pass, and all will be forgotten and forgiven."

"No, not this time, this war is unlike other wars, for technology has given our armies the chance to do what other armies of the past failed to do—and that is annihilate the enemy completely."

An elderly woman entered the hut and offered Genji a cup of warm tea, which he graciously took and drank, and then said, calmer now, to the elder, "And what about your village, why are your people still here?"

"The army has come through here."

Genji shook his head and displayed a hard countenance. "The Japanese high command does not want any Chinese left alive, and that means second waves of troops coming through to find those civilians who got away. This is not a war against the Chinese government—we don't care about Chiang Kai-shek and his forces in the south or the Guomindang and the Communists in the south; we are here to exterminate your people—your people are the target, not the soldiers; your villages, your cities, your children—not just army bases; your schools and hospitals and churches, your culture, your history, your race—any place there are Chinese, our bombs made by good and devoted Japanese men and women citizens will be dropped and our soldiers will come in and make sure no one is left alive." His face, a radiant heat pouring off it, was shaking and his body trembled from the force of his passion.

The old man looked upon the youth with admiration and compassion. "The sins of your countrymen can only blight your heart if you march with them."

"But I have marched with them and betrayed my ideals; I have studied history and philosophy and I know that what I was doing was wrong; I should have fled Japan years ago but I did not have the courage; I am neither hot nor cold, and it is men such as myself who are more dangerous to the world, for it is our kind that good people might consider a friend, but we will only fail them in times of crisis." He looked at the pretty young woman who was using great solicitude to dress his wounds. "You are very gentle; I would not want to think that any brute might touch you…"

The young woman looked up at the village elder and then to Genji and then said in a soft whisper, "I was here when the soldiers came through."

Genji frowned. "And they left you alone? Why, that is a mira…" but he had stopped because he saw in her face the glimmer of personal pain and suffering even a proper Chinese woman could not shield. "No!" Genji shouted, and he bent down before her and prostrated himself and began to weep, saying, "Forgive me, forgive me, forgive me…"

But she lifted him up and, using her lithe fingers, dried his tears and sat him down again and continued to tend to his wounds, and then said with words that came from her magnanimous heart, "I am alive, and it is men such as you who will stop this war."

Genji looked to the village elder, his face pleading for succor. "My blood is on the faces of every Chinese, every Filipino, every Korean—and on every nation in the free Pacific Ocean and every nation in free Asia—and on everyone, everywhere, who feels the horror of tyranny in their free hearts and minds; this war, this terrible, terrible war that will never end."

The village elder said, with great certitude, as if he had already been there, "This war will end soon, Genji, but this is hard to imagine; but all wars end—when you are old you see the cycle of war and peace and know what precedes and what follows—and already this one is won; even now our valiant troops are draining the Japanese army of its power and will allow the Allies to win battles against them—and the Allies will need our country to make bombing raids on Japan; soon, the Japanese will leave us and we will rebuild and we will become stronger; it is the same when a bone is broken—that it becomes stronger when it is healed; it is the same when a man is faced with great adversity and overcomes it, he becomes stronger; this war we did not want, but it is here, and we will overcome our enemy and remain a great people; it is the way of the world, for one nation to rise against another, but only a weak nation collapses completely; but we shall never collapse," and here he smiled as he lifted up the chin of the young woman, who was now shedding warm tears, "we are too ancient, we Chinese; we will always be here, and we will be stronger when the next nation decides to invade us; and so in this way, perhaps, one day nations might hesitate to invade a country that cannot be cowed."

"But I cannot think about that now, for you are the oppressed, and I am the oppressor—if only I could regain my lost honor."

"You cannot regain that which you never lost, Genji; but if you want to live a better life, live as a citizen of Freedom and Love and Truth."

A young man burst into the hut then and bent down and whispered in a frantic tone to the elder, who then rose up and said, "There is a Japanese patrol coming."

* * * * *

"There are ten soldiers coming down the western trail," said the young man to the elder as they walked outside the hut; his voice was devoid of hope. "And there is a group of soldiers behind them, maybe sixty men, and there are troops a mile behind us."

"They are looking for survivors," the elder said.

"Your people must hide!" Genji cried. "I will stay here and try and gain time for them."

The fifteen remaining people of the village had assembled outside to hear the news from the elder. "We are surrounded; we might hide from them, but once they know we have been here and living here, they will come for us; once they know we came from other villages to occupy this one, they will look for us."

"How many rifles have you?" Genji asked.

"Ten rifles, three handguns, and one hundred rounds of ammunition; we can hold off one small patrol but nothing more; there is nowhere left to go."

A defense perimeter was set up and the men took up their positions and waited; Genji took up a position and waited next to the elder, who turned to him and said, "You must not kill your own kind."

Genji looked at him and said, solemnly, "My own kind would not murder and rape and pillage; my own kind is gentle and kind and loving. If my people become monsters and do great harm to Innocents, then I become their executioner, for I am no longer one of them."

"No," the elder said, and motioned to one of his men, who came up from behind Genji and grasped him mightily and brought him back into the hut and tied the struggling youth to a sturdy and stout wooden pole that was solidly anchored into the ground; it was from here that Genji, frustrated and struggling against the ropes, heard the fierce battle between the opposing forces; he did not know how he did it, but in a moment he was free of the bonds round his wrist and he flung his self boldly and fearlessly out of the hut.

The firefight was over; six of the villagers lay dead and all of the soldiers of the small Japanese patrol were dead. Genji ran up to the village elder, imploring, "You must let me save you now, you must! You cannot stay here and fight them and win and you cannot hide from them; they will hunt you as if you were—but you are to them—wild beasts of the field!" He looked at the many dead and he turned again toward the elder. "I will save you."

The words of the elder rung in the smoky air like the death knell of a sealed fate. "We are lost."

"No!" Genji shouted, looking to the western and eastern directions from which more troops would surely come, and he walked over to one of the fallen soldiers and picked up a rifle and held it on high, and then cried out with great fervor, "With this," and he pointed to his head, "and with this," and he pointed to his heart and nearly whispered, "and with this," and he remembered the soldier from whom he had stolen life but who somehow had given life to himself also, and he felt the glow of love and brotherhood begin to fill his empty soul, "I will give you life—as one other great man gave me life— this I will do for you, and gladly lay down my life for you—for I love you," and looked round at the survivors, "yes, I must love those who love Freedom and Truth and Beauty no matter where they are and no matter what army of darkness they face, I will stand with them—for such people compose the greater good of the world, and without them the world would surely perish." He came up to the elder and nearly pleaded, "Listen to me and you shall live. I know the mind of these savages— yes, savages—I know them because I have lived amongst them although I was never one of them, and so I could scrutinize them and learn their primitive ways."

"You are Chinese, today," the village elder said, graciously, holding the shoulder of the youth, "you are a citizen of the world—so speak."

Genji explained the ruse and the people understood immediately and then each of them scattered to the woods until only the elder remained.

"Genji," the elder said, "you will be remembered."

Genji smiled. "I will return," he said as he rubbed the human waste from the cage onto his clothes, "for I am a superior man, and a superior man might outwit even an army of brutes," and then he rolled about in the dirt.

The village elder embraced him and the two men shook hands, and then the elder too departed into the thick membrane of the jungle deep; and as he ran to the rendezvous point, he heard the explosion of bullets coming from his now-dead village.

* * * * *

When the larger Japanese patrol came running up to the village, they beheld Genji running wildly about and shooting like an unleashed madman at lifeless Chinese bodies and stabbing them with the bayonet at the end of his blood-soaked rifle and shooting rapid fire into the huts and screaming and yelling like one possessed of fury and vengeance who was practicing the delicate art of being a proper Japanese soldier.

The company commander, upon surveying the scene, shouted orders for Genji to halt his manic behavior and stand before him.

"Private, what has gone on here!" the commander shouted, as if he were ready to execute anyone who would not impart to him a satisfactory answer; the war was going badly and those in charge would suffer the details of failure with their life.

Genji, having already torn at his wounds that had been tended to, presented a bleeding and bruised, tissue-swollen, clothes-torn, dirty, stinking mess.

He was standing at strict attention and saluting with a rigid hand and proffering a face that radiated pride and honor. "Sir, defending our homeland from the yellow peril!"

The commander looked about and with a stern countenance yelled, "Tell me what happened here, soldier!"

"Sir," he began, in a voice full of fervor, after handing the commander his safe passage home orders, "the ship I was on was sunk by enemy aircraft and I was taken prisoner by these Chinese swine until one of our brave patrols came and then I escaped," he pointed to the bamboo cage, "and joined in the battle and killed them, I killed them all, sir," and he turned around and spat at the corpses of the villagers and then turned around to face the commander once more, but then he suddenly fell to his knees and bowed his head and allowed his arms to fall at his sides, "but I have failed, Commander, I failed to save the lives of my courageous comrades and have brought dishonor to my family name and my unit, and I wish for you to take my life," and bowed his head even lower until it fairly touched the red pool of blood that littered the place.

The commander had been looking about and had already sent scouts to verify the story of the soldier and to look for more villagers; and then the scouts came back and told him that there were no signs of survivors and that someone had been inside the bamboo cage for many days, as evidenced by human waste and blood and tissue therein; and the heart of the commander was moved by the sudden realization that the soldier in front of him was not only a hero but a humble soldier who was not satisfied with simple acts of valor but only with complete victory. "What is your name," he said, without malice. He nodded with pride painted across his visage when he heard the name of the soldier still kneeling before him, as if the sound of this name had a special meaning attached to it. "Arise, Private Haki." Genji did so. "You are to be honored for your acts of heroism here today; you have done well."

The patrol from the easterly direction came upon them and the commander of this troop immediately was seized with suspicion of Genji's story and intimated that there must be Chinese citizens from this village in the nearby woods; the commander who had first found Genji, who outranked the other commander, was outraged and suggested that the commander apologize to Genji, which, suffice to say, for an officer who had been in the act of dolling out life or death orders to his men for years, was very amusing, and he laughed, until his head was separated from his neck by the silver, sharp sword of the other commander, who now held his red-stained sword on high toward the other patrol.

Presently, Genji was on another ship, and this time he had new orders that would allow him to stay an indefinite period in Japan until he was healed and well enough to return to combat; but as he convalesced, his obvious predilection for interpreting human action and his genuine affability gained him a job as adjutant with a high-ranking government official, and there he remained until the war was over.

But when the war was over and the final two bombs had been dropped and the final rendering of the final dead and wounded presented, Genji felt the weight of being alive, perhaps through subterfuge and perhaps through cowardice and perhaps even through betrayal, crush him; he was Japanese and yet he was a man but he loathed what his people had assented to and still he could not separate his genetic inheritance from his emotions; he wanted to leave Japan and live anywhere else on earth but he felt the umbilical cord of the mother country pull him fast and plant him like the roots of a very old tree; but he could no longer endure the idea of existing with his own people while considering what he had done during the war, so one day he simply went to the newspaper and bought an advertisement and made a full confession of everything he had done during the war.

The next day as he walked to work, he was pelted with food, he was covered with scorn from head to foot by his neighbors and by his friends, and never did he run from them or anyone else; he was nearly run over by motorists and struck by citizens as they rode bicycles past him; when he arrived at his work, his boss terminated him; when he came to the home of his fiancée, she closed the door upon him; when he went to buy groceries, the grocer would not serve him; when he went home, the apartment manager had thrown out Genji's belongings, and never did he hide from them or anyone else; and as he walked along the street and pondered his fate, he thought to himself, "But I am a free man now."

But people are not creatures who can hold on to malevolent thoughts for too long—well, most people will not, which leaves a savage group who will always hold a grudge even when they no longer remember what their maddened ire was originally directed against; and so, Genji soon found a nearby city to live in and another job and another girlfriend, and in a year's time, he took out another advertisement, which gave a full confession of all that he had done during the war; and once more the people scorned him and heaped abuse upon his head like burning coals; and once more he moved on until he found a place to live and a job to work at and a fiancée to love; but always he would make a full confession in the local newspaper and then the citizens of his city would drive him out; ten years later he was in yet another city and with another job and another girlfriend, when once more he had printed his war exploits in the local newspaper, but this time there were few stares and few comments and even fewer people interested because they were prospering and moving forward and yes, seeing in him a reflection of themselves; many strangers came up to him and he became their father-confessor, as they confessed horrible things they had done during the war. "So, here I shall stay," Genji decided, and he did stay, and made a great fortune in the real estate market.

There were two items he always included in the advertisement he would post every year of his life: that every year he would return to the village in China where the people had been so kind to him, and he would revisit the island where he had killed; and so, every year he went back to China and lived for a week with the villagers who had found him on the shore, and he went back to the very trail whereon the Allied soldiers had been forced to march for so very long.

When he was a very old man, and a very rich one, and a very famous philanthropist, he returned once more to the village in China, and then he returned to the scene of the long march, where others had also come to walk along—veterans of the war who had survived, children of veterans who had survived the march and who had died, and people who just wished to inspect this geographical area that had become symbolic of Man's inhumanity to Man.

Genji was walking along the road with his wife and his grandchildren, and he was explaining to them what had happened, and then he came to the exact spot where he had seen Frank attempting to leave; here he had been many times and yet now he stopped and stared in a westerly direction, and he murmured to himself, "What did he see that others could not see, what did he know that others did not know; what did he have in his heart that others did not have, what did he understand that others could not understand; and why, why was he unafraid to die—how could that be—how can any man not be afraid to die, especially a man who is so young?" And he began to walk on the same path as Frank had so long ago. "What possessed him that gave him comfort and joy despite the hatred of those around him? What would the world be like if there were more like him?" And he presently stood over the spot whereupon Frank had died, and Genji knelt down and caressed the verdant grass and soft soil. "What kind of man am I, Frank Petrocelli; am I a man as good as thee?" And then he realized, at that precise moment, he had sought to be like the man he had killed, and indeed had become like him; and he wept, and looked again toward the golden horizon Frank had beheld. "It is Love that you understood, Frank, it is Love that possessed you, that protected you and took away your fears; and it is Love that will protect us from more long marches." He looked toward his family and then looked again to the spot where Frank had fallen, and his breath was like a sweet fragrance that soon caught the soft breezes and flew to places where oppression of people lives, and his pleasing words were like a healing salve on the wounded hearts and minds of those oppressed. "He knew that Love is stronger than hate, but he knew that hate could kill only the body, and not the soul; Frank knew this and he was unafraid to die; for he knew where he was going and knew he was righteous in the eyes of God; lo, how this world has fallen from the exquisite garden we first encountered, how we have wandered far from the idyllic land we first inhabited, to an alien world that veils what is the proper way to live; O, Frank—who gave me life that day, so that I might live and give life to others; and in this way it was not just a death march but a march of life for some, and for those now who understand it and behold its terrible fury, they might hesitate to cheer their leaders who declare war on another nation, for there will be only more unbound hatred and more long marches and more graves dug with rancor and wrath and more widows and children who will mourn their fallen dead." He stood up then and smiled toward the westerly direction and nodded his head and then walked back to his family and took the hand of his loving wife and continued on the walk along the route he had so long ago traveled, a journey he would never finish.

-Finis-

The Autograph

In his dreams, lucid and bright and unceasing, he was not merely the dark, brooding messenger of doom, but the incarnate slayer who visited every victim and smothered their existence with a large expulsion of rancid air from his black lungs; he would sweep in from a darkened sky that was exploding with his image in a multitude of bloody, screaming, malevolent shadows, and enter into their bodies, into their consciousness, and live all of their lives, experiencing their every joy and hope and sorrow and fear. He would then move about, in that thundering, blasting moment, and engage their blood, tissue, and sinew, depositing upon them little drops of future death that began to leak and disrupt the harmony of their bodies; for others, after devouring their history, he would spread, like an oozing, volcanic fog, over their skin and burn them into dull, ashen heaps, letting powerful fire-winds catch their pitiful remains and sprinkle them over the land; and from these sooty bits he heard their wails, their sorrows, their immutable horrors, but he continued on, for there were so many more to incinerate, so many more of their memories to peel away, so many more vital juices to be drained from their struggling bodies. Those at the beginning of his journey were the quickest to be consumed, and he would pounce upon them and simply erase their visage or inhale their body and then staple their bewildered shadow to a blistered, cracked wall. He became a master sculptor, carving gargoyles from boiling, dripping flesh that was stained with red blotches from the moist radioactive dust and then depositing the carcasses onto towering mounds of bleached white bones that formed towering letters. He was compelled to cremate and burn and rip and kiss their screaming flesh off their crumbling frame—and he was engorged with the horror of it, the injustice of it, the cowardice of it. A communion with his senses occurred then, bringing the burning stench into his nostrils, and he retched and pleaded for abatement, for he was not the designer of this holocaust, nor a willing participant; yet, the more he remonstrated, the faster his mighty wings moved and the faster he continued to destroy the fleeing, stunned populace.

When the countryside was properly split asunder and wiped clean of vegetation and the buildings scorched or melted or simply blown to chunks of burnt molecules, he rested above the terrain and observed the piles of the dead, focusing his eyes until the grotesque letters formed by the corpses were apparent to him: Geoff Franklin Low.

He would awaken then, seized with sobbing and panic.

* * * * *

This nightmare, which occurred every night, was like a perpetually regrown and diseased organ in his body, spewing forth toxins and shame to deplete his heart and soul and mind.

"To sleep is to die in pieces," he often whispered upon awakening, his slim body drenched in sweat, his mind trampled by a pounding, rapid heartbeat.

His wife would not talk about the dream anymore, for she had realized long ago that it was his burden alone. "He is the only one who can free himself," she would say, bringing little solace to herself as she felt his quakes and quivers on the cool bed.

And she would weep, quietly, away from his pain, a monument of pain she could never share.

One day, in the twilight of autumn, when the brown and yellow robust leaves are struggling to be free, and the world is cool and lazy and content, she found a letter on the glass table. The writing had been done with a great urgency, and stated simply, "I am gone to find the deathless hour."

Her tired old eyes shut for a long while, for she was imagining him purging his haunting there. "You will yet live, my darling Geoff," she whispered, tenderly, and she cried then, for she knew that his salvation was at hand.

* * * * *

He was old. His face evinced a kind of accelerated and weary age, one that preserved the disillusions and disappointments of life; his eyes, cobalt blue, and atop the high-bridged nose and the eternal frown, stared desperately out of the window of the plane. He tried to calculate, with his scientist's mind, where this country's regional airspace began, the point where he would be susceptible to the wrath of the people's omnipotent collective consciousness, which was incessantly on guard for the creators of the Thing.

He could not, however, delineate the exact dimensions of their invisible airspace, and so, in terror, he closed his eyes and waited for the airplane to land.

It was the face of the coward, amassing waves of grimaces and frightened expressions, that the pretty airline stewardess saw as she approached him.

"We are in Japan," she said, quietly, reassuringly, and detecting his sobbing, was careful not to mention him in particular, "and all passengers must exit the plane." His pained countenance became a flurry of anguished panels painted with exquisite strokes that formed a vivid mask that momentarily froze and pleaded for mercy. Her genuine smile, however, was one of a bountiful nature, broad and etched in security and familiarity, and she used this honest weapon to allay his fears and, presently, to escort him off the plane.

Perspiration pooled on his dry skin and soaked his smart uniform that the culture of the dress-for-success people wore, those citizens who heaped multicolored threads upon all kinds of sometimes pleasurable but mostly undesirable-looking flesh; but this drunken blue he wore, this smoky shower of shocking blue attire, could not, however, cover up the walking grave of its human owner.

As he stepped into the white taxicab, it seemed to him that it was a sentient metallic beast eager to nail him inside its leathered belly and cover him a with a black, gooey rain and digest him until only his feeble, pale heart remained, at which time, he imagined, his flabby organ would be passed to the citizenry and nibbled on for eternity. On the foreheads of the people he saw his signature, the bold signature of a grinning, arrogant young scientist who had promoted himself up the ranks on the death and crippling of millions of innocent people.

And he could not close his eyes for fear that his internal torment would deliver a more fearful crop of grotesque images.

He felt himself shriveling into a wounded little boy who is now lost in a forest so dense with wild growth and shrieking shadows and terrible noises that he cannot, even for a moment, find time to engage equanimity of mind and follow the path of light to safety. He was their prisoner and they did not know it.

The city into which the prisoner had delivered himself for execution was replete with the microcosmic world of all cities, containing all of the elements to survive and flourish.

It was a city of modern invention, and it had the soul of the jungle, an environment where each species had adapted to survive in its little niche. Here, the businessmen collected power like beads on a string, and so they needed to be housed in a monolithic shell of steel and concrete, which emanated, though falsely, prominence and safety and superiority. These merchants were the queens of this nest, watching carefully over their obedient workers, the drones, who had adapted to a life of submission and groveling. The customers were like grains of pollen from the fruit of the tree, feeding the insatiable appetite of the colony.

He envisioned none of this; instead, he saw only a city mangled and laid open like an oozing sore and attended to by vultures gorging themselves on the charred remains of the dead he had helped plant in the cold ground.

There was a sign posted, proudly, defiantly, atop the entrance to the skyscraper hotel he now stood in front of, and it said, without pain, without sorrow and ostentation, "August 6th—Survivors of the Atomic Blast—Reunion."

He commenced to babble like a baby, right there on the sidewalk, in the midst of thousands of citizens who were walking briskly to and fro and thinking of job or family or food, thinking of destination and joy and fear, not once thinking of this old American male who was fragmenting to pale, brittle bits; for they did not care, had no time to care, and did not see him nor distinguish him from other events; for in this atomic forest, one saw all manner of life and its immediate consequences, and this man's crying jag was as inconsequential to them as an old derelict prostrate on the ground or an old dog sitting there with a drooping tongue and sad eyes who pathetically struggles for life. He was simply a mass of matter taking up space, and people merely moved one way or another to avoid him.

Once inside, he would not take the elevator, so he stumbled to the emergency stairwell nestled inside the building.

He stood, bent over, like an aged tree laden heavy with snow, unable to extract himself from the fresh, glossy smear of waxy shine on the tiled floor.

To make a step upward would signal an inevitable union with what he considered unbearable emotional pain.

"It is better to sit," he decided, and he fell in a crumpled heap and gained a momentary reprieve. "I am a member of an ancient civilization," he whispered, gasping, gaining no comfort from the embalmed air, "who has been separated from his time, his tribe, and set to wander amongst a finer society that would seek my death for atonement of my sins; it is good, then, to die now, for I am weary, and my burden too great to bear," and he proceeded to crawl up the stairs like a wounded soldier.

As he conquered the cement steps at his languid pace, he felt a weightier burden upon his head, causing a heavier breath, a louder beating of his flailing heart and a blurring of his vision.

Approaching the halfway point, he encountered a small, solemn figure who was adorned in a long, flowing, white robe and who stared down at him with the utter dignity of the Japanese spirit.

"Do you seek," the figure said, quietly, easily, "to dissemble the truth in one continent and assemble it in another?"

Geoff lifted his bilious face and stared, bewildered, unable to speak.

"Do you seek to build a citadel upon the forgiveness of the undead and the dying?" the figure contended.

There was no reply, only a helpless, forlorn look.

The figure bent down and set his head closely to Geoff's wrinkled countenance. "Life is continuous motion," he whispered, and he interlaced his slender fingers together, "unbroken and undisturbed—it is like a stream near a shore, every molecule of water one thought of your life, where every action is a movement; and it goes forever, irretrievable," and he stood up slowly and placed his words carefully. "You cannot step in the same stream twice."

Geoff managed to utter a reply through a parched, inflamed throat. "I do not understand."

The kindly man smiled. "This is because you have not lived; you have only existed."

Geoff bowed his head to drain his mind of a horrible fog that prohibited him from engaging this man; but when he looked up again, the enigmatic sage was gone. "Well, of course, it is my malady," he said, urging himself to subscribe to this conspiracy, and he moved onward and upward, extending his elbows out to grab the floor and pull himself up, raising his skinny legs to help push himself to the next level.

He lay dormant—sprawled like a man who has just crossed a battlefield and has gained a foxhole—on the small landing platform. Soon, though, he had generated sufficient energy to continue the quest, and fought the next step, conquered it, and then continued upward; but then a hot, swirling vapor engulfed him and, upon looking up, he saw the same noble

Japanese man, who graciously bowed and then moved his hands about the frosty, wet spray of the mist that now began, in its bosom, to evince a series of events.

"Why," the nameless figure inquired, politely, "were you created?"

And behold, Geoff witnessed his birth in the whirling, silver fog.

Geoff, his mind bewildered, then took up a bundle of abstract thoughts and swallowed them whole and separated them until only one very strict, very disciplined idea remained, and then he replied, "A union of male and female."

The Japanese man smiled. "The reply of a true scientist—yet it is the same with all who live but who do not question the past or present but clog the atmosphere with their annoying presence and unconscious acts of stupidity—but no, I do not seek a biological explanation; for what purpose were you begat?"

Geoff's faculties for advancing his apologetic stance were paralyzed by Truth that was now seeping from all of his tissues and into his pores in a regurgitating, tarry, bubbling stream that was slowly suffocating him. It was this current of Truth that began to flood the staircase below him, impelling him to drive upward to the next level. His Guide had absented himself from the scene once more.

The frothy sentiment spilled from his skin like a gusher as he rose, like a worm, slithering to the fifth-level platform, which he quickly passed to reach the next step, all the while driven by an urgency to find the esoteric Guide.

The fog descended upon him again and this time, within its ebullient nucleus, a series of vivid moments from his life presented themselves to him.

"Why," the sonorous voice began again, and there, above the fog and Stream of Truth, stood his Guide, poised in midair and adorned in a regal splendor of discipline, civility and humility, "did you so greedily gulp the oxygen about you with a violent passion—why?" and he pointed to a portrait of Geoff's youth in the swirling mist, a rusty-haired, skinny lad with an abundance of freckles who was engrossed in investigating scientific phenomena and busily dissecting machines and family radios and building workable lasers and making amazing discoveries with his chemistry set.

Geoff felt a smile peep through the pollution of gloom and pain that was growing like weeds in his gut. "Youth," he heard himself utter, purely, humbly, "let me suckle at your breast and feel the pulse of innocence and freedom—this is good," and he spied his Guide, confident that his Mentor would nod approval.

But it was the voice of a master condemning his slave.

"You are dead in the flesh and the spirit."

And behold, a large, opaque hole, resonating a weird chorus of howling melodies, appeared above Geoff and descended upon him as it provided a gooey, milky-white lubricant dripping from its mouth.

He began to shriek as the churning orb enveloped him, first by his sparsely populated head of white hair, and then slowly munching the rest of him until at last, he was away from his present physical universe.

He was born again.

During a two-minute moment of accelerated time in the present space-time continuum, he emerged from his mother's womb and soon again was the curious boy who wreaked havoc upon his home with his ingenious experiments.

The two minutes in real time expired and he was sent back.

He lay, prostrate, with a whimsical smile upon his happy visage. "Send me back," he said, fondly. "I want to live forever there, in forever land, safe and happy and free."

"You are a child now," the Guide said.

Geoff lifted his gaze to his Mentor, and said, "I do not deny it; I cannot survive this world, so many mistakes I have made," and he hung his head low. "Send me back so I can live in peace."

"You would change everything?"

"I would deny all of it to be free," he whispered, and suddenly his contentment was evanescent, "and to have peace."

The Guide merely shot out his right arm to point to the next level; and, at that exact moment, the Stream of Truth raged out at Geoff again, and once more he attended to ascending the steps with his crawling, crippled whine.

He did not rest on the sixth platform but rushed to the next step and moved onto it, still feeling the now-syrupy, chocolate-colored spring gushing all about him, engulfing him like a sprawling virus.

"Your life," the Guide said, in his easy, poised voice, as he appeared on the steps above Geoff, "is without scrutiny or discernment. You must learn by amplification and not obfuscation." The roiling hole appeared again, and his Guide shook his right hand at it. "Now go, and live your chances."

* * * * *

Geoff lived again from birth to graduating from the university with degrees in physics, chemistry, and biology; he published twenty-two articles in prominent scientific journals before he received his PhD in physics at the age of twenty-four; and then he had an offer to teach at Harvard before his twenty-fifth birthday. He lived it slowly, leisurely, with only one singular unifying thought extracted from the future, and it was this: that his great scientific knowledge would inevitably lead to a great holocaust.

He came bounding through the purple haze in the stairwell, headfirst, young still, and then he aged rapidly, causing him to look back in sorrow, witnessing his supple, sleek body sag and wither, until, finally, he was old again and stricken with regret and tasting heavily a wine of gall. "Curse this life," he whispered, and sank into a profound depression.

"You think you are reborn when you cross the time bridge, but it is when you come back that you are truly reborn," his Guide said, solemnly.

Contempt, like a mountain of rock, had established itself upon Geoff's face like a monument forged from the elements of hatred, bitterness and envy.

"I can teach you nothing," the Guide espoused, disappointment flourishing about his visage, and his disappointment soon transformed to disgust as he raised his now purple-silken-robed hand and pointed upward. "Now go."

The Stream of Truth broke through the natural and temporal barricades of innocence and again began to chase Geoff up to the next level, though he was cursing and muttering stray and rambling discourse that was aimed at a world that had peeled him, layer by layer, as if he were a soggy onion; and when this excavation was done, only a dry, dull husk of a man exposed to the harsh judgments of history and society remained.

"I want to die, here, now," he groaned, crumpling in an exhausted heap upon the third step of the next level. "Give me a sword so that I might fall upon it."

"You boast of amending past errors," the Guide returned. "Relive the passion that lies, now, rotting on the fragile vine inside your heart."

Geoff fell into the deep recesses of melancholy. "I fear that I possess two minds: one a captive of the past, a prisoner of the moment, the sum of all my experiences up to that moment and dedicated to executing the right thing; and the other, now, but I am morose and unable to prevail against my other self, who, if enlightened about my present self, would shudder and curse me."

"You must experience the defining moment, you must engage it, taste its savory juices that drip with the formless, timeless, polished power of extinguishing life with a thought," the Guide said.

The response was soft, penetrating, exhaustive. "No."

"You cannot deny the past; you were part of the team."

Geoff closed his eyes tightly as if to shut out a horrible truth seeping in. "I cannot," he whispered, but the terror contained in his cells, anchored like a steel ship, shook, and he felt its choking, scorching presence. "It comes," he roared, tremulous, his visage stricken with a pale sickness, "the Punisher, enslaving me in its filthy, gauzy web, entombing me with a venomous injection of spite and obscene poetry that recites its lustful hymns in my mind," and here he savagely beat his head and then pulled his lithe, yellow fingers through his hair, "and I cannot exist without it."

"You were happy the day of the Signature."

"Shut up," he cried, and he turned his head as would a child, who, once obedient, now becomes enlightened, "you shut your dirty mouth." The words did not so much come like ordinary speech, but rather they were assembled in a dark factory in his mind and exploded along a slick track to his thin lips that, once whetting themselves with the proper lubricant, tipped the verbal bombs with the flaming fuel of hatred against Truth, and blew them out like heat-seeking missiles to their target. "You'll shut up or I will shut you up." No addenda were necessary now, no flowery speech, no floral bouquet of adjectives to stress this naked attack; he merely expelled his sentiment as he lay, rigid, bitterness devouring him in huge gulps.

"You would change the Hours of Triumph?"

"Yes."

"I will assist you, Geoff Franklin Low. Behold."

The Nightmare realized its entire masochistic, loathing self, right there in the concrete corridor, loosing a ravaging spirit upon Geoff.

Geoff disgorged the horror he had kept locked up within himself every day, and had lived every night in his dreams.

At the Nightmare's end, he swept up to his Guide and reached out his hands to enwrap the Guide's neck in a passionate embrace; but as he did so, the Guide transformed into a charred corpse that emitted a blue, smoking, acrid fume, a burning flesh fume that purchased Geoff's nostrils for very little and ransacked his brain. Undaunted, Geoff strangled him, cursing and shouting and promising destruction to his tormentor as his fingers squeezed the crumbly, stringy neck and soon became smothered in its odious, oozing lather.

The Guide began to emit a howling, screeching clamor from his yawning mouth, a hideous mouth that stank from his scorched and decaying internal physiology, a wide cavity that began to suck Geoff in, first by his head into the vast chamber of inky darkness, then by pulling the rest of Geoff's shaking, wriggling body totally within its warped borders.

* * * * *

He was there again, now, at the momentous signing, and he was fully armed with all the knowledge of the future.

The nickname of the bomb was "Little Boy," and it was ten feet long and twenty-eight inches in diameter, weighed nine thousand pounds, and it was going to make everything good again. It was the great equalizer; it was going to bring a marvelous submission from the despised enemy and save blessed lives and end this long, unclean war and reunite families all the world over and bring a balance to nature again.

The target area was good because the people were inhuman and their leaders were inhuman too and they had refused to yield and they were all guilty under the laws of God and Man—at least, everyone seemed to think so; the enemy nation had refused to yield to the forces of Good and Justice and Common Sense, so they were going to get it, good and hard, get it in the soft gut, and they would yield to the almighty American Atom, the darling of the ingenious physicists, the newborn child of scientists who swaddled her enriched uranium in steel casing and prepared her for a brief sojourn to the future city of the deep graves.

Geoff was young and vital and surging with righteousness, and he knew the future.

"We will save lives," one of his colleagues said as he picked up the thick, black pen and carefully posted his signature on the metallic shell of the bomb. "It is for our boys and their families; we cannot sentimentalize it."

The Nightmare pounded against Geoff's thick skill like a thundering hammer that gave birth to new hammers that bored into his cranium and beat in a constant rhythm that signaled the cry of the future's undead.

Here he was, his two states of mind—regret and righteousness—comingling, and he felt the ripe urge to go forth with the signing.

"This is war," another said, gravely. "We must do this. I don't wish to, but I must; it is a good thing even though it will bring death and suffering."

Geoff, in his mind, sought a way to persuade his fellow scientists of an alternative plan.

"The destruction," someone uttered. "There will be such utter obliteration."

"There," Geoff thought, "a fellow doubter, a renegade, yet!"

"For every minute we waste time debating this issue," an elderly scientist began, "my son, your son, our brother, your brother, our neighbor, our friend, an American, a citizen of the Free World will die; a million Allied troops await the signal to invade if we do not drop the bomb. Think of all the soldiers who will die; think of all the soldiers we can save if this bomb is exploded over the target area; think of all the civilians who will live if we do what we know is right." But even he could not bring himself to call the target area by name. "Think of all the future families who will exist because we have crushed the enemy with a single blow."

Geoff was ready to sign, but then another scientist intervened.

"What we have wrought here," he said, his voice quaking with a portent of doom, "will begin the race to build greater bombs of mass destruction."

A young scientist said in a tormented tone, "And why a city..."

The elderly scientist replied, his visage grim, "We cannot worry about the consequences of our actions for the future, for then we would never proceed without uncertainty. No, we must go forward and do what needs be done now and worry about tomorrow another day. Gentlemen, if we do not drop the bomb, we know this to be folly; so, I say to you, we must do that which we know is right now and have no regrets about it."

Geoff, in a trance, signed his name on the polished metal that would dig the graves of generations. "It is done," he mused, trembling, and in an instant, he was back in the present.

There were no noises now, no Stream of Truth, no Guide now, no illusion, and no uncertainties.

He raised himself from the cool cement surface and commanded his sweaty body with power and urgency up the steps.

There was a knock on the door of room 415A, a forceful knock by the American scientist, and an old, stiffened, balding Japanese man politely let him in, asked him to sign the guest list, and escorted him to the main gathering room, where five hundred survivors of the bomb sat in purple, glossy metal chairs while listening attentively to the woman at the wooden podium. She finished and there was no applause, for one does not applaud the scars of the past that teach the world about suffering.

Geoff walked right up there, unscheduled, unknown, and stood before the brown podium and looked out at the bewildered people, who checked their program for a list of speakers.

He would not think about it. He would merely execute it.

"My name is Geoff Franklin Low." His voice was firm and brave and determined. "I was one of the physicists who designed the atomic bomb that was detonated on your world." He was still brave, even in his delivery.

His words were like hot, molten lava dripping slowly, intermittently, onto their burning faces.

"I signed my name on the atomic bomb like one does on a tree with one's lover; I wanted to sign it with all my soaring heart and soul and ripe young mind and body, and we sent our lover to you, and you knew her intimately." A low hum, like wind coursing across a grave, began to grow. "I am not here to explicate my actions nor grovel like a kicked dog for forgiveness—I am here because I hate war as much as a human being can, and when there is war, people die and suffer." He paused, looking around at the stunned audience.

"And when does one forget?" he said, passionately, looking around the silent room.

"And how much time must pass?" he then continued. "Shall we curse those who warred against our ancestors? What are we in the machinations of fate but a transitory flutter in the great expanse of the universe, manipulated by the accumulative events of any person in the past who contributed to the manifestation of the war? Shall we curse them, too? Then we must curse the ages, the air they breathed, the water they drank, the bounty of Nature they partook. We are all," and here, for a moment, he smiled, inwardly, as he intertwined his fingers, "inextricably woven." He saw their faces, filled with revulsion, but he would not think about that now, and said, "We must move on after we bury our dead, and for those who suffer still—emotionally or physically—why, then, I say to you," and he felt a chill of sanctification encompass him, "love one another, as I love you. For if we hate, or fear the past, we live buried in the past, in a shallow grave—a shadow—part of the Undead."

After all those years of unceasing torment and this five-thousand-mile journey, he was done in an extraordinary, one-minute flurry; but he was free, free to move without the corroded iron shackles of the past digging into his raw, bleeding psyche.

He expected nothing and, in fact, received nothing as he walked straight out and down the purple rug and past the aghast survivors to the huge yellow door and out to the carpeted hall.

Then, from the meeting, a small woman came up to him and embraced him, and uttered in her native language a single, emotional sentence, and then turned and went back in, weeping.

He felt a quiet murmur dilating his heart, a murmur of love and respect and forgiveness. He cried then. "One," he whispered, and smiled, and he went away, never to return to this place.

-Finis-

Of Greater Significance
than Mammon

He was stumbling, tumbling, moving in a lopsided manner; he was lurching low, crawling, urging his body to go forward; he could barely see because of the blood, he could barely function because of the tremendous loss of blood, he could barely think because of the holes about his person through which his thick, cold blood spewed so precipitously.

He should have been long dead.

There were too many wounds in too many places for one man to sustain and live; yet live he did, albeit awkwardly; yet live and give the sword to pain he must now do—this pain that was gangrene on his plans to reach a geographical point by a certain time and be in a certain physical shape; and still he fell and crumpled into a tangled heap but then elevated his impossibly alive body once more, his mind purchased by a singular thought, compelled on by a distinct vision, fueled by a noble desire to bring succor for others without any benefit whatsoever to himself—and that, he knew, was a new creature in him, the old one having been plucked and crushed and winnowed down until it had seen the birthplace of self-lessness in the glowing embers of natural freedom; yea, he could smell liberty now, much as he might have inhaled the pleasant odors of autumn, he could taste it in the viscous fluids that streamed down his swollen face, he could; he could hear the ripe tunes of it in the echo of gunshots still reverberating in his ears, he could; he could see it not in his blurred vision but in his recently resurrected heart—resurrected by the betrayal of dark forces, who, when they step away from their fallen victim, reveal even more the bright and shining light of Truth and Justice.

But in the end there was simply too much of the vital life-force being let out of him—like a punctured cup releasing water, it flowed—and he would faint and fall down; but somehow, in some superhuman, superhero private viewing chamber, he could see himself down and out, having lost this last and perhaps only sacred quest—so, he might be down but must not be out, and urged himself awake, rousting himself from unconsciousness with newly acquired, stellar companions—Virtue and Pride.

He had been a master thief, a supreme artist at his craft—ars celare est artem—fooling his birth family, his friends and his relatives, and his colleagues at his regular employ; lo, he even concealed his exact methods of handiwork from his fellow thieves, and by doing so, contracted from them—like a disease—their gushing admiration and enthusiasm for his quiet and unassuming, cold-hearted, precision-like labor, and he had even acquired a hitherto-unheard-of honor from his nefarious playmates regarding his expert craftsmanship while enriching their overflowing, golden, jewel-encrusted coffers; yet, none of that mattered to his masters, those who considered themselves his betters, nor even to those who considered themselves his equals, or even those who knew they were inferior in the esoteric, smoke-clouded realm of the criminal class; and yes, there are even societal strata—like strata in tall rock mounds—that are unyielding and uncompromising in this alternate universe, and clear customs and values and creeds to obey, too; and now he had violated a fundamental commandment as he met with a superior, to wit: he had unequivocally, absolutely, and undeniably refused to execute this order: kill his family.

It must be explicitly stated, and emphatically so, that when a subordinate is given an explicit and emphatic order, there are no questions asked by the underling, no options begged, no tactical stalling or hemming and hawing, just a quick nod of the head accompanied by a calm visage and a quick exit to evince they have an eager spirit to please; and once the dirty deed is done, these inferiors are to make a swift return to their superior and issue a thorough report and an expressed desire to carry out even more commissions, whether the jobs are difficult or not—for all jobs have the same ranking for the junior officers; it is just another job to do, and nothing more, nothing personal in it, no interest taken in it beyond what was necessary to complete it—period, finished, done. But this man had refused immediately, without even asking why his family was to be killed; he had not even inquired if there was another way to handle the affair or even if another assassin might handle it; nor had he even paused to see if the order was issued merely to test his loyalty and would never have been carried out; no, not him, for he had, in no uncertain terms, even with a bald bravado, enunciated clearly and succinctly to his two bosses, that no, most decidedly no, impossibly no—not even— anything but that, no—just no, I refuse, not even stating the obvious rejoinder that he had been loyal to the gang for ten years and had never refused them—ever; and yes, he had even poured more boiling gall into their already overflowing cups by promising—yes, even promising, even boasting—that the order absolutely and positively would not be carried out; and yes, to cinch the noose he had created with his incendiary words even tighter around their fat red necks, he most decidedly and with the utmost vim and vigor assured them that if anyone else tried to fulfill the contract he would, without any reservation at all—as clear as fine crystal, he told them—stop any and all who were involved in it and then kill any and all who had ordered it; and then he had just stood there with that machismo look on his rugged face, as surely as if he had just challenged two ordinary men to an ordinary fistfight.

And though one might even back away from a relatively innocuous confrontation, there was no backing away from this steel gauntlet he had not only thrown at his masters' heavy feet but had first viciously slapped across their flushed faces; but still further, it had to be resolved there and now and not in a moment outside or after a long drive in a car and certainly not on some dark roadside, but now, right now, for the glowing embers of wrath were melting the resistance of the men to wait.

And so they did not wait.

The two betters pulled their pistols first—pistols as common to them as black plastic combs to ordinary men—but it was ineffectual—as they surely knew it would be, but were forced by pride to try—for the man before them was a consummate professional and had faced all manners of men in every kind of situation; the two betters fell in a hot flash, and their two personal bodyguards came rushing in from the outside with guns drawn, only to offer a last devotion to their bosses by dying and then unceremoniously lying atop them; but the alarm was sounded now and the entire den of thieves was aroused, and when they saw the carnage of their lone fellow, they became like anxious hounds full of the scent of the hunted fox, and eager to chase and fetch for their sanguinary masters.

Yet now he was a thunderbolt in a dark cave, and he was caught rather quickly, and wounded, and beaten and then taken to his commanders, who tarried not, but rather shot all about his person with their mean weapons.

One would surely presume that a merciless soldier checking the presumed war dead would make certain they were, in fact, dead, and might even fire volleys into bodies that appeared to have a glint of life; but a lazy merciless soldier might just walk past someone who portrayed all the bloody characteristics of someone who ought to be declared null and void—dead; and so it must be stated now that this is how the captured man looked, with some twenty bullets puncturing his muscular frame; yet, had they checked, as they hoisted him aloft upon their shoulders, they would have detected that low-emitting and still viable spark that is life, still within him; and here, he had three courtesies of fate bestowed upon him: one, that the two men who handled him mostly had been his closest allies—men who had deliberately missed with their guns as they had so energetically chased him about the big mansion, because they had owed their lives to him on multiple occasions and had never had the chance to offer him recompense; still, there were other men who handled him but the man's macabre appearance led them to believe that what they handled must be a corpse; but here is the second miracle that allowed the immortal breath of providence to pass over the man—he had been in the last war and had been wounded in combat and had had special space-age metal alloy plates placed in his skull that had partially blocked the bullets so expertly aimed at his delicate brain; and the last player in this short script from the testament of destiny involved a special material he was wearing that was even unknown to the other unrefined gentlemen, clothes made of a space-age material that generously and assuredly slowed or altogether abated the progress of the most irksome of high-powered projectiles.

Still, he was a bloody mess, and unrecognizable to his former colleagues, who, except for two, reckoned him to be a traitor and now fodder for the slimy worms; and the bosses decided he was to be deposited near the home of his family, so that the police would forever ponder the link between his death and their massacre.

So, here he was, pushing his sinking, bloodied form along the cold, snow-covered ground, knowing by the terrain and the merry sounds thereof where he was; but he never lasted too long upright, and most times fell and crawled, or knelt, as his body hung limp like a man dangling from a rope; and few cars whizzed on by—for it was a desolate region of town, a place he had personally chosen to raise his family in and protect them from... criminals; and it was the heart of winter and there was hoarfrost on the ground and it was shortly after midnight; still, the cars passed by him just as if they were robotic cars devoid of life and not cars with humans inside who recognized the plight of the man, but upon seeing his dire condition, begged off and denounced the weird vision as something they must not soil their precious hands with.

Alone he was, now, shuffling along, and when he did manage to stand, he tripped, and when he managed to walk, fall, and when he managed to crawl, it was on bruised hands and knees, and done with a desperate desire fueled by his need to protect the only living things in the world that gave him spiritual sustenance and emotional calm and love and joy—his family; it was a superhuman effort, but he knew his own superhuman strength, and knew he was finally beaten as he lay there feeling as if he were covered in thick layers of sticky goo while being crushed by a mountain of gigantic boulders.

His pierced and pounded body was still, his mind was adrift, his energy waning, and hope was flowing out of each bullet hole and into the icy sheath that covered the rocky soil upon which he lay. He had failed and he knew it, and this was worse than any bullet or beating he had ever taken.

Then came a stranger, and a new light shed its warm hope upon him.

It was curious to see how the passerby, upon seeing the wounded man, did not ponder or look about himself for others, but merely, like the pull of electromagnetic forces, went straight to the man—or perhaps more like the pull of the natural forces of brotherhood; as it was, the passerby attended to the man without reluctance and with compassion and worry, just as if he were caring for his own: showing no fear, and even an ambitious attitude to aid the downed man.

The wounded man, with a strong grip, took hold of the stranger's thick, black coat and said in a desperate voice, his bloodied, passionate face aimed upward, "The men who shot me mean to kill my family—there," and he nodded somewhere in the direction of his home, "1427 Kimberly Road—they are there now to kill them," and he reached in next to his back belt, wherein was tucked the black Colt pistol one of his sympathizers had surreptitiously placed there, and took that wicked weapon and reached out and felt the empty hand of his rescuer and slapped that cold, hard steel into it and closed the hand with both of his. His voice was sodden with desperation when he murmured, as if truly the lives of others depended upon the sincerity and veracity of his words, "My family will die if you don't go there now and stop these murderers," and then he fainted.

The passerby stared hard at the man and then looked up through the misty air to the small, wooden house, wherein a light was burning dim in the white-curtained window, and then looked down to the man; and then he stood up, still staring at the man and hearing the unbridled passion of his words as he lay there; and so he instinctively turned to address the physical reality of the house so he might register the importance of it to the man and then looked upon him as if he might find answers therein and suddenly felt an indomitable spirit of courage bore up within; and presently he found himself walking toward the house in the same manner we are drawn to any awaiting human catastrophe where we know if we do not attend to it, it will come to fruition.

The navy-blue house was shrouded in a sooty veil of darkness, having been set far back from the street and the nearest streetlights; he approached it as if it were a mysterious package that had recently appeared at his doorstep—with great circumspection and the acute edges of a magnified fear; he unhitched the wooden latch of the white, wooden picket fence and walked through the gate and stepped lightly on the unusually long cement walkway, looking all the while up to the screen door and expecting it to open and someone burst through it and explain it all to him; he could not, as he walked up the grey cement steps, pull himself from this moment, this place, this journey, as if somehow all of it made sense, even though he should have simply gone for help and called the police and by doing so kept his humble nose low to the ground and out of other people's business.

As he lifted up his head and gazed upon the house, he did not understand why he was here; he knew that there was no compelling reason to do this, no real reason to be here simply because a dying man had directed him thus; and what if, he now thought, as a chill rippled up and down his lean frame, the man was right and the criminals were already inside the house or maybe on their way here. He knew that he shouldn't be here, but here he was lifting up his hand and the next thing he knew, he was knocking hard on the wooden siding of the blue doorframe.

Presently, he heard commotion inside, and he knew the game was afoot—the door opened just as he placed the blood-ied gun behind himself and tucked it between his pants and muscular back.

A pleasant-looking woman opened the door and threw out a quick smile and said, "Yes, may I help you?"

It struck him now that he had not thought of what he might say had someone actually answered the door—would he speak the truth or would he lie; if there were men inside with guns, what should he say; if there were not men with guns, what...

"Yes," he said, frowning, "um," he stammered, studying the countenance of the young woman for emotional upheaval, for a break in the continuity of a daily ritual that might impart to him a clue, but he saw none. "Well, I was just walking along the street," he began, and abated his sentence, not certain whether to say the truth, and he looked deeper into her pretty face but saw only a placid calm—and this worried him, as he was a stranger very late at night and she should have elicited at best a glimmer of worry or at least a hesitation to come to the door or truly should not have answered the door at all; however, he was here now, and he knew if there were men inside, he was now trampling on their sticky, murderous web. "I found a man." As soon as he uttered this he knew he had erred, that in its stead he should have said, "I thought I heard someone scream inside," or "and I was looking for a friend who used to live around here," or anything other than the stark truth.

"Yes?" she said, again, her visage still smooth and eerily quiet and absent of panic at the midnight appearance of a stranger at her doorstep.

Now, he was sweating profusely and beginning to tremble. He wanted to run, to flee like a frightened little boy who has poked his big nose way too far into the forbidden zone and who then runs home and climbs into bed and pulls the sheet covers over himself and makes all his trepidations go away.

"Well," he began again, feeling that with every imprecise, stumbling dive into attempting to create a coherent story, he was presenting an improbable and untrustworthy image to her, "who seemed," he could lie about the man, but if the man really needed help and he let the man die because of some silly story, "hurt..." There, he had said it and he could not take it back, and now he waited for something solid to materialize that would enlighten him.

And then it did—a big, big, very big and scary-looking man with a powerful build and meaty face came to the door and said in a sympathetic tone that seemed forced and given life just for a brief, uncomfortable moment, "Yes, what man?"

He knew he was dead now, that he had ruined it now, that the dying man had told the truth—for goodness' sake, he thought, feeling nauseated and sick as he felt consumed by the seemingly growing sinister countenance of the man inside the house, why would a dying man lie, and why, he reasoned, would any man allow his wife to answer the door this late at night while obviously listening to the conversation between her and the stranger while he stood in the safe veil of stealth? Think fast, he mused, or die young.

"Well, he was over there," the youth answered, timid still, pointing in the general direction of the dying man's resting place.

"Come in and I'll call for help," said the large man with the skull that looked like it had been chiseled from a square block of solid white marble.

This man gave me an order, he thought as he walked nervously into the warm room, and he seems too eager to bring me in.

"Oh, my name is Scott Bloom," the behemoth said, extending his hand as if it had just occurred to him to do so, and then shook the stranger's hand. "Here are my brothers—Hank and Johnny, and Lester—and my wife, Joan."

The youth shook their hands and felt relieved that perhaps he had been mistaken.

"Hank and Johnny—why don't you go and check to see if you can help that poor man outside—and you," he said to the youth, "why don't you sit for a spell as I call for the police." The big man walked past the tall green fir tree to the phone and dialed some numbers and spoke briefly and then hung up the phone. "Help is on the way—say, is that blood on your shirt?" His voice still seemed cordial but it had a bit of wild energy dancing around its periphery, as if there was a force trying to break into his processed and pressed tone and burst forth and evince its true shocking colors.

The stranger looked down at his shirt and pants. "Why, yes, he was bleeding badly."

"Bleeding badly, you say?" And now the tone of the man had attracted a weird sense of urgency that seemed misplaced and beyond his role as helpful citizen. "Was he conscious—I mean, did you talk to him?"

The youth thus felt unease strike its fearful sharp-edged sword into his aching body again. Why is he asking—why? he thought, should he be asking such questions? But as he was so musing, he noticed that the man—too big, too ugly and mean looking to be married to so small, so pretty and gentle a woman—was not wearing a wedding ring; and then the youth was furtively glancing about the neatly groomed room for evidence that would render a quick verdict, which he soon found in the form of a golden-framed photograph of two people—husband and wife—standing together as they were cutting a tall, white cake at their wedding—and in this picture was most certainly the clear image of the woman but not of the giant, and maybe, just maybe it was the exact image—even though it had been dark and only for a fleeting moment—of the dying man.

"Well," said the youth, trying not to step onto a verbal landmine, "I really..."

The next thing he knew, he was being tackled roughly from behind and laid flat on the plush white carpet.

The giant cursed as he walked over to the wedding picture, and after picking it up, tossed it casually to the ground. "I didn't expect visitors—at least not now; the police later, sure," he sneered, his face obviously revealing the joy of shedding its temporary veil of congeniality that had strained him so, his voice filled up with a ghastly vapor as he stood next to the supine man, "to identify the bodies." Now, he smiled, like the spider that has trapped its nightly meal and is anxious to wrap it up. "Let's see what we can see, eh?" He bent down and let the full extent of his unusually strong body odor engulf the youth as he frisked him. "Well, well, what is this?" He nodded to the two other men and they violently yanked the youth upright, and then he held up the gun directly in front of the face of the youth and said, as if he were sipping on a vial of hot steam, "Are you a cop—punk?"

He had been a wiseacre his entire life, this youngster, a wisecracking wit, a son-of-a-gun who used words like small firecrackers thrown into the gaping mouths of unsuspecting victims with their dull visages and vacuous eyes. "Let me guess," he said with a slight shade of cockiness smeared across his handsome face—because he was so relieved that the truth was out, and now he could be who he really was, "you're not family, are you—or maybe you and your garrulous brothers are just a tad overprotective." Now, this was an acceptable piece of witticism to be fired like an incendiary shot in an innocuous verbal joust, but completely out of synchronization with the hard tone and theme of the perilous night, to wit: he received a hard punch to his hard and already flexed gut, producing little ill gain for the big man's searching ego but confidence for the youth.

The big man, with the face as if it were cut into a candlelit giant pumpkin, grunted, "You little punk, where did you get the gun, huh?"

"I found it," the youth replied, feigning agony still, authorizing the use of his intellect to weave a story so full of guile and temptation for his rude host to want to believe that the resultant explosion would blow a huge hole in the adhesive property of this villain's monstrously drawn web; he finished with a sheepish grin, "in a crackerjack box." Came another punch to his gut, and again he feigned dissatisfaction, but he reckoned it worth the trial; and then said, as if to appease his captor because of his own physical torment, "I found it near the man," he began, in a forced panting and gasping, "and no, I am no cop—however," he said, louder and stronger, as he straightened up, "I am a proud citizen of this fine country, and I am hereby making an official citizen's arrest of you and yours, as is my right." And he stood, his hands outstretched toward them as if he held imaginary handcuffs, as if he expected his antagonist to be amused, too.

The quizzical look on the face of the walking-upright-lion-but-masquerading-as-a-man fell, and then he produced a small guffaw of incredulity and a hard curse. "Why, if you ain't the little smart aleck," he said, tapping the brown butt of the pistol against the head of the youth, "don't you know a mouth like yours can get into a whole load of trouble?" But then the temporary civility in his voice dropped away like it had been sitting on a putrid piece of flabby voice-skin, "Like getting your head blown off when you meddle in other folks' business," and he pointed the black barrel of the gun to the head of his hostage and pulled back the trigger.

He knew it was extremely important to upset the man's sense of equilibrium to gain the crucial time he needed, and so with a cool mind and calm voice he said, "Too bad you won't live long enough to get that Criminal of the Month Award you've worked so hard to earn."

A look of incredulity and shock compelled the ogre to release the trigger on the pistol and then smite his thighs with it. He exclaimed, "Boy, you just don't know when to stop, do you? Why, if you were my son, I'd tan your hide every time you talked such nonsense," he cried, irritated now, "and 'specially when you're about to have your brains scattered all over this nice lady's fine carpet—for shame."

The bemused youth let out an amused "Humph," and then said in an assured tone, while on the inside shaking like a baby in the cold and the dark but on the outside cool as one with a lit match next to a short fuse leading to a pile of dynamite upon which his enemy sits, "And what will you do when your boys come back with only excuses?"

"Huh?" the big man replied, hoisting the gun up once more toward the youth's head, but then his two adjutants came bursting in from the back door to announce they could find no body anywhere, and that, incredibly, a blood trail they had found had just up and vanished.

The youth nearly collapsed from the profound relief this news bulletin brought him. The first miracle is done, he thought, and now I wait for the second and third, and he peeled back his senses to explore a path that would produce an explosive and fast-moving conflagration.

He had quite forgotten about the woman—clearly, he knew now, this was a mistake, for if she were the wife of a man who was formerly near death but now somehow was walking about and perhaps had been an associate of these ungentle men, she just might be familiar with living a violent life, and might offer some clues as to the survival of herself and himself and her small daughter, who was playing quietly on the couch with her doll; so now he looked to the woman and saw that she was not so demure looking and timid as he might have expected a young housewife to be—she had a taut and athletic body and she looked strong of character simply beyond her straight body posture and lifted-up head and cool demeanor, as if she too comprehended what was next to come. He waited until the big man with the deep-set black eyes and wide red mouth and bulbous nose turned his ruddy face elsewhere, and he gave a barely perceptible nod of his head and then formed with his lips as she scrutinized him with all of her life-forces, "The gun." She gave a barely perceptible nod back, this silent wavelength just grazing past the glance of the big man who squinted and frowned as he attempted to retrieve the communication between the two hostages.

"What do you know about this, eh?" he shouted at the youth, and then, turning toward the comely wife, asked the same question with a grotesque foreboding of imminent punishment scrawled across his pockmarked face, even as he moved toward her to immediately fulfill this prophecy.

The youth was frantic now, looking everywhere for the second and third miracles, and when he saw them, he felt that delightful blast of adrenaline surge throughout him and elevate his body into the realm of great strength and his mind into the cavity of great will and daring; as the big man raised the pistol to beat the unflinching wife, the youth said, calmly, as if he too were holding a weapon, but one of an immensely greater intrinsic value, "I know where he is."

The big man abated his forward progress and looked back to the youth, and the three henchmen gazed upon him, too. Good, he thought, I have drawn all of you to me. And then he said, slowly and succinctly, "Behind you," and then he steadied himself for the ensuing cataclysm as he looked to the wife and whispered with all his mind and body and soul, "Now."

All four members of the criminal underworld looked, albeit briefly and cautiously, to the back door, but upon seeing nothing and turning their now-angry stares once again to their trapped game, found that their insular world had suddenly and completely been instantaneously and irrevocably altered, to wit: the formerly captured and sedated wife, even before yelling to her child, "Get down, Charlotte," had now transformed into an adroit soldier versed well in the various disciplines of hand-to-hand combat; first, by bowing the big man with a swift kick to his groin and then simultaneously grabbing his hand that held the weapon and turning it so quickly and harshly that his grip was relinquished on the still-bloodstained pistol; and then she, with her free hand, liberated him of the gun, and subsequently sent two successive bullets into his massive chest—so, down one, and three left.

At the same instant in space-time, the husband, being the second miracle, he who had resurrected himself from the iron fingers of the grave, appeared in the front doorway, pistol in hand, being the third miracle, and hot lead screaming through its short, black barrel.

The youth, as he fell to the ground, out of the corner of his eyes saw the infant vault herself up and over and behind the sturdy, steel-reinforced grey sofa, just as if she had performed this stunt many a time; and then he slammed against the soft carpet and closed his eyes and covered his ears and just waited for the cannon fire to cease and hoped the proper people would still be left standing.

It did not take long, truly, it did not, for when six marksmen are engaged in mortal combat at spectacularly close range, a critical decision will be rendered with the greatest expedition; and so, in the moment it would take to pick up a dropped book, all was decided, and peace reigned once more in this small home.

He opened his eyes; the unharmed wife was kneeling over her still-alive husband and then spied that the four members of the local crime consortium had had their permission to terrorize innocent folk revoked. "Charlotte," the mother kindly bespoke, while holding fast her husband's wounded body, "it's all right, baby, the nice man will bring you to me now," and she looked knowingly back to the still-sprawled youth, who presently stood up and walked behind the sofa and saw the little girl with the blonde curls hugging her dolly; and then he whispered, reassuringly, "It's all right now, Charlotte," and he carefully picked her up and cuddled her close as he walked around the bloody corpses and then bent down and delivered the precious cargo to her parents, and then walked over to the phone and did what was necessary, and then stood far away from the family so as not to invade their private world.

"Elaine," the man whispered to his sobbing wife, "I have done many bad things, and often without regret; but now, I have done one good thing, with regret it took so long; and no man alive will ever harm you and my baby while I yet live—whether as a good man or a bad man, for even a bad man understands Love and knows he cannot live without it."

She was caressing his bloodstained face and wounded head when she said, tenderly, "You were always a good man, my love; you just had to learn it."

And then he, who had precious little energy and words left in his magnificently perforated body, looked beyond his family to he who was no longer a youth, and said, with brotherhood and profound reverence, "Good Samaritan." The man, who, out of respect for the family, had not looked toward them, did so now, and they looked at him. The wounded man then uttered, with great solemnity, "You have given my family a great gift." He paused, and smiled, as he nodded, and held his wife and daughter close. "You are the man I wish I had been."

The wife whispered a fervent "thank you" to the man.

The youth smiled faintly and nodded.

Sirens could be heard in the far distance. Snow was gently falling outside. It was Christmas Day.

-Finis-

100

There was flat land and barren soil and a two-lane highway running right through the heart of the empty desert. No machines or life-forms could be seen in the darkening sky above or in the pale ground below. The place was dead and sterile, dead and wiped clean by something, dead and unnaturally washed by a catastrophic force that had left no trace of its awesome power. But here it was, this perfectly drawn, perfectly laid-out highway just sitting there like a long, black stripe down the back of a sleeping cobra.

Next to the asphalt road were many bald-headed men, each of whom was attired in the same beige-colored, long-sleeved cotton top and long pants. Their faces were grim and their words were harsh as they surveyed the eerie calm around them. They stood in groups of five or six, close enough to hear the words of their fellows.

"We do not have much time," one of them said, a tall, slender man with coal-black eyes that had lain too long in a raging fire; "we must decide now." A weaker man would have allowed a stronger man to utter words and thus capture the moment during a lull, but this man would allow no such thing. "We must attack it with ourselves. There is no other way." There, he had said what he wanted to say, and now he would allow others to embrace this idea and modify it and move it around and look at it from every angle they chose, but he knew now that his idea would be the one they would abide by.

A big man, a very big man with a long scar down his long face, discharged his booming voice into the sultry air. "He is right, we must use ourselves; there is no question now. We must act."

"But how can we stop such a powerful thing?" a slender man asked. "We, who are just flesh and blood, and it, which is fire and steel?"

"We shall hurl ourselves against its hulking mass and thus slow its momentum," one of the smaller of the men began, holding his head up high. "It is mere physics—and it will work if every one of we one hundred apply ourselves to the destruction of this thing without hesitation or mediocrity; simply put, every man here must meet this behemoth with all the available force in his human locomotion in order to conquer it."

There was no time to contemplate other ideas or utter expected protestations or capitulate to defeat—it was time to allow one's thoughts to immediately transfer out into the ethereal air and congeal into action; and still, the men, faced with such a weighty burden, needed to hear doubt expressed.

A small man asked, "But who am I that I can bring down such a mighty thing?"

"How do we know every man will do his part?" asked another.

Still another asked, "Should one man die for nothing if his brother is a coward?"

A tall man, who possessed large muscles and a mean look upon his sunburnt face, spoke with great affection. "No man amongst us is a coward, for all men here have come to this place for a purpose greater than themselves." He nodded his giant head in satisfaction as he looked about his assenting brethren. "We will have no more talk of it. It is not for us to worry about our failings but mediate upon our strengths, and this is what we are—men of strength."

The last remnants of light were erased from the sky as darkness descended upon them. The men instinctively looked upward and sensed the urgency of their mission. Still, no sound was heard about them, no squawk of the bird nor howl of the coyote nor rustle of the lizard on the flat ground.

One of the men bent down and scraped off a thin layer of the beads of yellow sand that had been fused into a weird, smooth glass. He had not spoken until now, but now every man looked at his every movement and waited for his every word. He rubbed the bits of pitted and pimpled sand chunks between his long fingers and then dumped them back onto the hard surface. He stood up and walked over to the strip of asphalt and stood upon it and looked down its great length for a short duration and then turned around and faced the men who had been closely watching him; and when his deep voice uttered words that were wrapped in a smooth cadence and a confident tone, every man there yielded to him.

"We are not men who can likely forget what we have done, but who can now atone for our past; it is the way of this world that men such as we, who have been condemned by our own actions, might find redemption before we die; it is a good and noble thing we are about to do, and it is the only thing we must do, for it is the proper and righteous thing all men must do when the destruction of innocent people is nigh; we cannot fail in our attempt, for failure means there is no justice in the world, and we, ourselves, by our very actions, know this not to be true; so, we who once perpetrated injustice shall bring justice to a world that is better without us. It is an irony we might consider had we lived." He expelled a long breath and nodded his head as he looked upon the captivated men. "This day, by our very deaths, we will be like other men, and it is a great sorrow that we might only obtain such honor and glory this way." He turned round and stared again down the long stretch of black asphalt that disappeared like a mirage into the sinking black horizon. "Each man must be a precise tool and attack this beast where it is most vulnerable," he said, his voice in a trance-like state as he walked along the asphalt, the men close behind him. He gesticulated about, pointing to various areas of the road. "We must purposefully and skillfully strike it at its weakest points; every structure has such things—every dam and doctrine, every building and bridge—even Man," and here he interlaced his fingers, "has a certain point where even the strongest construct fails; yes," he nearly whispered, pointing ahead now, "we shall strike him high and we shall strike him low, we shall strike him in his iron belly, and yes, even on his iron nose," and when he punctuated this with a flashing fist, the men cheered. "Yes," he began again, starting to run now, and the men with him, "we shall apportion hurt to him as he would do to our own, and we shall stand over him with great authority and power and smite him."

He crouched down in the middle of the tarred road and peered straight ahead. The men crouched down all around him, too. "He will come fast, very fast and very certain that nothing will stop him, so nothing we do in the beginning will rouse him from this conceit; so, my good brothers—and what are all of you now but my brothers?—here is the plot which will lay down this mechanical beast for all eternity." The men listened as he, like a master weaver, wove a master plan that spoke to the very heart of these anxious men.

So, every man was ready now, every man at his appointed station and waiting for the first faint roar of the metal monster. They were sitting on both sides of the road for a quarter mile, each man rehearsing what he must do, each man rehearsing what his courage must do, each man rehearsing what he must accept to abrogate the sins of his ignoble past.

And soon it came, a tiny thread of noise trickling down from the boiling air, and as it landed on the men, they felt a sudden chill sweep over them and arrest their calm; some of them attempted to dismiss the sound as desert chatter that was spoken by living creatures, but they knew better; and when the roar of sound shrapnel began to prick the air with its sharp claws, they knew the moment was upon them. They could feel the hum in the vibration of the hard-packed soil, an unmistakable sign of unnatural power that Man had loosed on this planet.

The clamor grew louder, and with it, the resolve of the men weakened. The men were drenched in perspiration and fear.

The man who had designed this strategy cried out in a voice of equanimity and certitude, "This is our moment, brothers, and we must not fail those who must live and carry on what good tidings are left in this world! Courage!"

This steel behemoth was thundering down the road now and the desert seemed to shake and tremble and bow before it. The men the furthest down the road were the ones who were the heartiest and bravest, the most foolhardy, the most angry, and it was up to them to light this fuse that would ultimately explode with the last of the men.

Now it came, crashing and pounding and hammering the blacktop as if it were the only thing in the desert and the only thing that mattered, boasting of its powerful structure and speed and that nothing here nor there nor anywhere else could impede its forward progress.

It came into sight. The men at the forefront sneered and nodded their heads and they spied the mighty titan barreling toward them. "Come and get me," one of the men said, and he tensed his hard muscles and watched intensely as the thing crept closer and closer until the moment of collision was upon him. "I go," he shouted, and the men all about him felt their chill swept away as they spied him springing toward the huge vehicle.

It was a flatbed truck of truly epic proportions and power, being composed of a shiny black hood that was built of the finest metals and contained the finest engine for speed and strength, and a long, ebony bed that had a small, oblong object securely tied down to it with steel cables and iron chains.

The first man sprang up like a panther right into the reinforced windshield, but he merely bounced off it as easily as a grasshopper would have. The driver inside grunted and sped on toward the goal. But this first action of the man had set off the rage of the other men—rage like a hundred mousetraps exploding one after another in a small wooden barrel—to move out against the truck. The second man went, and he thrust his body up and out and into the thick window, but he too bounced off it and then he too lay dead upon the road. The third and fourth men jumped into action.

These men dove straight into the underbelly of the truck and were caught up in the long, cylindrical drive shaft and were chewed up atop the big, black sets of hot tires. Four more men moved against the truck, two high and two low, two men up against the windshield and two men straight into the carnage of the drivetrain. They hit their target and died and then the next set of men moved swiftly.

From either side of the road the men came in waves, in twos and threes, hitting high and low, then in fours and fives, hitting low and high, every one of them hitting their mark and every one of them dead after their daring deed. Half of the men were gone and the truck was still blasting down the road as if nothing but insects had brushed against its great bulk; no damage had been done to it, no mark could be seen on its sturdy glass eye, no crack could be detected in its churning underbelly and spinning tires.

Ten more men launched themselves with great force and speed against the truck and found their immediate objective, but once more this attack had no discernible effect upon it. Ten more men went against the truck and ten more men fell alongside it.

The truck had never wavered nor slowed as it approached the last of the men. It looked the same, except that there were human remains strewn across its steel shell and poured underneath its long bed. The last of the men now leapt into action.

The next six men who hurled their bodies into the convex glass window and the guts of the truck died never knowing that they were the ones who were to validate the labor of their fallen comrades, for after their broken and twisted and discarded bodies lay like mangled dolls in this withering chasm, small cracks appeared in the mighty windshield and puffs of black smoke now spewed from the whining drive shaft and differential. The next ten men could not have known this, but still they moved against the slowing truck with all the might and muscle in their missile-like bodies; and then, a small crack in the glass widened like a magical spider now spinning a magical web, splinters of the wound moving out like streaks and veins of lightning; and there, among the smoking drivetrain, came a great gnashing of broken pieces and twisted metal.

The last men beheld this revelation in the silvery rays of the moon, and now knew that it is in every small contribution that leads to victory; and so these men, thus enamored with this notion and strengthened in their cause, set out to do great harm to this beast.

So, they hit it high and low and they hit it good and hard and right into the heart of its injuries, and with only five men left, the once-seemingly-unstoppable monolith was limping and seizing along the road like a dying creature. The windshield was a mass of broken lines and shattered sections and the drive shaft was barely turning, but the truck would not relent.

The first man jumped high and set his bald head straight into the cloudy windshield and this action severed the remaining bonds of cohesion left to it and so it buckled. The next two men too directed their torpedo-like bodies into the decaying glass and once their bodies bounced off the hood of the truck, the glass was barely intact. One more man jumped.

He knew what the plan was because he had been the author of it, but he could not be the finisher of it; no, this would be left to another man. His body crashed into the cabin of the truck and fell against the screaming man inside. He rested against the writhing body and felt the wrath and rancor of the man with every struggle and shout. But it would do no good to resist, he thought, as he found the neck of the driver and concentrated on grasping it until the man no longer moved. He could not see nor cared to see, for his only concern was to wrest breath from the man, and this he soon did, and as he lay against the now-lifeless body, he could feel the truck barely moving, and he smiled then, for he knew that his brethren had won.

And then he died.

The truck came to a halt a little ways down the road, and the last man came up to it and quickly climbed atop its bed and placed his slender hands upon the outer steel casing of the oblong object. It did not take him long to disassemble what a few had taken so long to carefully assemble; and when it was over, he leapt down and slowly walked back down the asphalt road, and as he passed each man, he halted and acknowledged him and bowed his head.

And when he had come across the last man, he came back to the vehicle and took out the body of the bald-headed man and carefully laid him alongside the road, and then said, with great passion and sorrow, "And who will know what we did here but those who have died here; but I know, and I will bring honor and glory to you."

And he walked on down the road and soon disappeared from view.

-Finis-

Soul Love

He was holding onto her hand as if he were holding onto the entire world; his strong left hand gripped the slender, white ceramic rail of the boat, and his strong right hand gripped her left hand while her right arm swung free and her legs dangled over the screaming vicissitudes of Nature.

They were human beings yet were like flotsam in a shaken bottle as the ocean bellowed and belched in energetic paroxysms below them, drenching the man and woman in icy water and clamorous noise; the crackling lightning scratched the tarry sky and bleached it white and scratched zigzag patterns across its heaving bosom; thunder resounded like a million powerful cannons shot and a million explosive battles fought; the foaming blood of the earth raged and shook up and down and back and forth in her raging fury—like a mistress scorned, like a wife cast aside—and would not subside until she released all her frustrations and fears upon those who dared sail atop her tempest skin; and she had already swallowed whole too many and drowned too many more and wreaked havoc upon land, sea and air; she was a widowed goddess pouring her lamentations o'er the world, bearing the dead and dying down to the weeping jewels of her serene and cerulean-turquoise soul.

The woman was hovering above the churning spirit of the sea, feeling its watery tendrils wrap around her flailing legs and pulling her towards its briny, callous grave; but then she looked up to her beloved and cried, "My husband, let me go!"

He was straining now with all the physiology of his body; but then he cried to her, as if the stated purposes of the known world and its accompanying precepts were inferior to his singular presence, "Wife, can I let go of my own soul?"

"You must, David!" she cried, feeling the eclipsing power of gravity as it cast its steel raiment around her slender waist, "and live for us!" Her tenuous grip slid a barely measurable portion down his weakening hand.

"Rachel," he shouted, grief pouring out of his mouth like a stab wound, "can I live without the air I breathe?" His hand strength lost a tiny measure of inviolate human real estate.

"My beloved," she whispered, her expression born of love as she felt her body pass the delicate threshold of more down than up, more there than here, "you will always have me."

"My love," he cried, his face burnished by the golden aura of love and fidelity, "I have you now and always." His steady pull upon her growing weight waned.

"David," she murmured, somehow her meek voice piercing the clamorous roar of the perfumed caldron below, "have faith in us and I will be with you always." Fetters of heavy iron assembled themselves round her slim ankles.

"My life," he said, his words forlorn and dressed in despair as he beheld the roiling waves begin to lick the bloody tongue of the menacing wolf that waits for us all, "is your life."

Her long, blonde, soaked hair lay wrapped around her bare bronze shoulders like a soft cotton shawl. Her hand slipped a lifetime down his hand. Her voice was forlorn and dressed in despair. "My love is your love."

He saw resignation move through her beauteous face like a cancer as he said in a voice full of hope and certitude, "We can never be apart." His stamina was withered, his power ebbed, and he felt the world recede from him as she began to pull away.

She was seized by the last scattering of her will to endure and resist agony beyond unreasonable human limitations; and her countenance softened, and her aquamarine eyes grew in luster and radiance as she now saw only him; and then she said, as if it were a virtue just discovered and spoken with unequaled passion, "I," she whispered, projecting herself into his luminous brown eyes, "love," she murmured, as if her soul now beheld his soul, "you," she finished, as if their two souls had just come together and become as one.

The rhythmic beat, the musical chorus of this yawning, icy mistress below them grew louder, its sharp melody singing a beckoning song, its shrill voice humming a syncopated symphony; and now it rose up and enveloped the two lovers as they fell—united in mind and body and spirit—upright and embracing each other and gazing with absolute tranquility into the other's mind as if they were not presently midair and soon to be swallowed up flesh and bone and blood and laid to rest in the watery fortress of that unconquerable sovereign world below.

But lo, their downward-moving feet never touched a single molecule of white spray, their entwined bodies never felt the chemical bath of brine and froth and foam, their slowly turning bodies never experienced the cold immersion into this watery abyss; in its stead, they felt a pleasant warmth and now a passing quiet and then a pleasing sound as if crystal bells were tinkling all about them; and as they looked about, they beheld a wondrous and magical world.

They were floating now inside an embryonic fluid that maintained them and nourished them as they continued to gently spiral down; as they fell further, they experienced a feathery-soft cuddling upon their skin and a soft humming in their ears and a soft, diffuse light in their eyes; and they saw more embracing lovers falling down this translucent, shimmering landscape; and everywhere there were brightly colored flowers: deep Blue Chicory Flowers and White Rose Blossoms and Crimson Cinquefoils streaming alongside all of them and spreading forth a lovely scent; and the two lovers felt the gentle kisses of golden sunlight caressing their flesh and dressing it in a warm raiment; and never did they question this rainbow-honeyed, perfumed fairyland or worry about what was to occur, for their souls were cradled in the bosom of Tranquility and Harmony, in the very essence of Honor, in the rarified spirit of Fidelity; yea, they had come to reside within the sacrosanct borders of the House of Virtues wherein live those who have transgressed beyond the obsession of self and have eagerly sacrificed themselves to bring relief for others from the petty but sometimes profound sufferings of this miserable and sometimes wondrous world—a world where one might even die for sinners so that the scales of pride and arrogance and the intoxication of the flesh might fall from their defiant, lustful eyes.

They did not muse upon where they had been or where they were now or where they were going, but who they were now and why they were now and that they were together, now— and that was more important than being alive without each other for a very long time—even if now was only temporal; for now they knew that this blessed union was with Beauty and Truth and Love, and they knew there were few things more important in this world of suffering and sadness than practicing such noble Ideals.

When they happened to alight upon the unadorned ground, neither did they question how they had arrived there or where they were, but that they were together, and together made everything straight and clear to them in a world that was crooked and shrouded.

As it was, they were in the dappled and shadowed garden of their small, fenced-in backyard, on the very day they had intended to glide like the ancient mariner across the sunlit sea in celebration of their one-year union where their minds had dissolved into one common conscience and their hearts had dissolved into one emblem of love and their flesh had dissolved into one selfless vessel that sought to please that one harmonious mind and that one generous heart.

And so, they walked back hand in hand, heart to heart, soul within soul, now inside their humble home, to renew the starry fable they had created with Faith and Honor, and done so by cherishing one another and not by attacking the other; by not building one up merely to tear the other down; by praising what was good in another and not condemning the other; and so, they would continue to live in Harmony, championed by Love; and live in Peace, championed by Respect; and live in Joy, championed by Tolerance; and they paid no heed to what the world saw or approved or disapproved of; or how the world lived or did not live, or how the world rationalized its sins; no, for they knew what they had was real, and it was their special Love that made them real to each other, which made them whole and better able to combat this age of supreme temptation that urged lovers to do as they pleased and for as long as they pleased with complete impunity; and they did not care if they were the only man and woman in the whole wide world who lived as they did, for what they had was Beautiful and Innocent, and that was sufficient enough to protect them and sustain them and allow them to endure, and win.

-Finis-

A Purpose Given

He was nothing more than a homeless bum that you might see strolling down the road, with his long and thick, mangy brown hair and his faithful, mangy dog and his long, crooked walking stick and his dirty black knapsack slung over his stinking clothes. He was not unlike the bum you see who sits in the restaurant in the early and freezing morning, who is consuming endless streams of coffee that are poured with increasing irritation by his grumpy waitress; he was the same bum you see in the library, reading magazines and newspapers, and who absolutely and positively sits alone because his stench radiates past the sagging sofa he inhabits and slays any near passerby. He was exactly that bum who always seems to be alone and is always bearded and is sometimes seen mumbling to himself and is sometimes observed talking to things that are not seen by casual human observers. He was that bum, to be sure, the ubiquitous bum everyone thinks is either mad or drugged out or is simply not to be trusted or spoken to civilly—he was a bum, a character with no defined place in the hierarchy of society except to occupy the outermost shell, and in this distant periphery, he is welcomed, for here he is like the forager ant, the decomposer, the scavenger animal, and without him, the shreds and bits of society that drift away from the center and clutter the outer limits of society would pile up to the cerulean sky. Yes, indeed, he was that bum, indistinguishable from every other bum everywhere because they had all achieved the same rank and file in society—utter anonymity in the squalor and degradation of society's fifth dimension, the seen but ignored parallel universe of the outcasts and those buried alive but condemned to walk the earth as a reminder of what failure does to a man. It was the caste system here, just as in caste systems there, but the difference being that over there, they acknowledge it.

This particular bum had a name, Joe, a good ol' American name that had actually fit him well in his youth, as he was the Joe of everyone's idyllic notion—blond haired and blue eyed, humorous and humble, faithful and forgiving; he was going to be Joe whether or not his parents had named him that, for he was the embodiment of the American portrait of Joe, and he lived his name well; he had always seemed to do the right thing at the right time and always seemed to prosper even when everyone else did not, but more importantly, he was always there for anyone who needed his help and he would always, always, make sure they had at least half of his loaf of bread. He was, as stated previously, good ol' Joe.

He married young and married his childhood sweetheart— the best-looking gal in town—and in due time they were in the family way, with one baby born and another coming soon, and so the image of Joe continued to be painted with the majestic strokes of quiet and simple life, but now it painted his loving wife and beautiful boy and girl.

Put a man on a course that takes him to the highest highs and have him build a home there and let him dwell there for a spell and soon he will come to believe that this is life as it must be, especially if he has earned it by being selfless and noble and loving to his neighbors and family and friends. Joe surmised that he was supposed to be in this general vicinity of bliss and beauty, and yet he was still humble and grateful for every little thing he had because he knew there were folks who had less and who deserved more, folks he always considered and always helped in any way he possibly could. He was tall and handsome, strong and rugged Joe, and he never let anyone down.

And then one day—there is always that awful-sounding, apocalyptic phrase "and then one day" in the lives of ordinary people, but it is not supposed to be an appendage to the lives of special people like Joe; but here it was, and there it went, that horrible "and then one day," and the terrible something that happened to Joe was no fault of his own, nor was it anyone else's fault, and no one ever blamed anyone except the fates, or something else like that. As it was, it was a very bright and sunny spring day as he and his family were driving down the smooth road to the county fair when an oncoming car had a blowout and the driver lost control and it unavoidably and irrevocably smashed into the car that Joe and his family were in. Joe lived. His wife and children died.

But this is not entirely true. Joe died, at least the Joe the town knew. He did not merely come down the lofty mountain where his princely domicile had once perched, he fell off it and encountered every rock and ditch and thorn and sharp stick on the way to the hard bottom. He was finished, the people knew, the first time they saw him without his "shield that obscured his pain"; he was done; and there was no jealousy from the people, no glad tidings that this great man had fallen, for he had never been anyone to them except an exceptional human being, and they grieved for him and cast their net of sympathy and empathy far and wide around him; but he would not, could not have any of it, and although he was still very young and still very healthy and could very easily have started life all over again, he knew instinctively that he was done.

And so he left, and began to wander the earth as a restless spirit, wandering here and there, aimless, boundless, friendless; so, no, he was not the ordinary bum that you might see anywhere and who is dismissed with a haughty stare and given up for dead; and so the next time you see such a man walking alongside the road, you might consider where he has been and where he is going and what he still might accomplish.

Ah, but the story is not yet over, for Joe had still much to do, so we must accompany him on his sojourn and see what we can see.

Everywhere he traveled, he was searching, searching, looking for something he was not quite sure how to identify and something he was not quite sure existed, but his mind and heart moved him onward to look for this magical and marvelous something that would somehow ameliorate the pain and suffering of his lamenting soul. It was difficult to know exactly where to go to find this humming, whispering thing, so he just ended up going anywhere and simply looking at everything there was to look at—people, places, events, things—always hoping that it would leap out at him and be recognized by his tormented mind; he was not sure what would happen when this great epiphany occurred: he only knew he had to be patient and look for it all the long, tired day and all the long, restless night.

For five years he wandered the land, and he was surprised at how the citizens of his beloved country treated him; they stared at him and mocked him and hooted at him, and threw dangerous things at him and spat at him and cursed at him—and he having done nothing to them to elicit such behavior, either with profane language or profane conduct, as he was always the gentleman, always proffering help to the helpless or those in need, and often turned down even by folks who desperately needed succor. It was at times like this, when he beheld the cruelty of Man against his own kind, that he would feel the harsh environs more keenly, as if his profound sorrow and disappointment at his own species opened a wound in him, so that when he walked amid the moving house of silver droplets, he felt as if it were raining inside of him. He not only was on the outside of society looking in, he could not even get inside, and he was kept out by the very people who would have benefited from knowing someone like him.

Still, he was kind to animals, rescuing many a mutt and feline in distress, and he was kind to fellow bum travelers, helping many a wounded and lost man and woman regain their mental acuity; and still, no good deed he ever did seemed to qualify as that special something he was searching for, so he always moved on to the next town.

He liked to walk past elementary schools and see the children playing in the playground, for it brought peace to his mind to imagine his own children playing there; he was not like other men who are tortured by memories of the past, no, for he felt a profound serenity when he was deep in reverie about his family—they had been his fuel for living then, and they were his fuel for living now, they had been his engine for living then, and they were his engine for living now; it was their inviolate image that drove him to bring resolution to his quest; it was them, their pristine life, their joy, their laughter, their very existence that allowed him to want to wake up every gloomy morning and renew his pledge every cold night to find this elusive treasure; yet, he knew he could not stay too long nor get too close to schools, for the world of late had become suspicious of everyone and everything and saw conspiracies in everything and everyone.

He was aware that people stared at him, people in cars, people on the street, people in stores—they stared and they stared and they were not ashamed of this breach of common etiquette, for they reasoned that his station in life, being on such a low and distant rung, had no value nor place in the universal book of manners, as if he were the circus freak, the condemned criminal, the parading lunatic who was supposed to be stared at freely and without limit of time; but none of this bothered him, for he knew who he was and understood that the people back in his town knew who he was, and that his family, in Paradise, knew who he was, so he was not brought to anger or embarrassment by such untoward actions.

He knew he was a good man and no amount of condemnation from anyone could ever alter that.

He was an acute observer of all things around him, be they animate or inanimate, big or small, high or low, and he had learned to appreciate the variations in life as he moved from the country to the city to the forest to the valley to the desert and to the sea; he saw it all and took it all in and allowed this great diversity of life to form within his mind a kind of enormous tree: at the uppermost portion was the fertile crown, in which resided the thickest and heartiest branches and limbs, and produced the most beautiful and colorful leaves and honey-scented flowers and healthiest fruit: and these were the people who prospered and propagated without hindrance and often without an awareness of those less fortunate; below them were the thinner and weaker branches and limbs, with skinny twigs and faded leaves and flowers and bitter-tasting fruit: and these were the people who were born on the periphery of affluence and education; and beneath them lay the barren limbs and branches, and twigs swollen with disease that produced insect-eaten leaves and flowers and fruit that quickly withered and died: and these were the greater parts of the world who were conceived in the worst geographical places and resided in the massacre of war and pestilence; beneath them were the forked crotches: and in these were those too frail to keep their grip and who had fallen a little ways and now were allowed to rest before they quit this cruel world; and those who had fallen onto the forest floor were the ones who had willingly yielded up their spirit, but also those prideful and wealthy souls who had fallen from their lofty boughs, and despite incurring every kind of humiliation and suffering along the way, never understood where they had been or why they had been and where they needed to go, so they too ended up in this rot and filth of life's dismal failures; as for the enormous woody trunk, it was Nature: and it had the wounds of Man's ambitious mark upon it, and it bled profusely, and was doomed to destruction as it seemed there were not enough of those who cared to heal it; as for the roots: this was Nature also, the verdant plants and robust animals, and the clear cerulean sky and the sparkling blue sea, and these roots were now shallow and polluted and starved for oxygen from Man's industrious pursuit of luxury and leisure; and lo, the rich and powerful elixir Nature had once produced was now diluted and foul, and most of those who drank of it reasoned it adequate and never knew how rich and powerful it had once been; and yet, despite all of it, despite this horrific vision he had slowly and meticulously acquired, he saw himself as a strong and human bough that sometimes caught those fleeing souls, those abandoned souls, those wayward souls and gave them direction and hope and understanding—he believed he could do this because he was aware of the Tree and could be free and happy anywhere on it and knew how to survive without hurting it—so they might seek to live and flourish and once again regain their place on the precious Tree of Life.

So, he was thinking about this magnificent symbol of existence as he was walking along the thoroughfare near an elementary school, when he happened to see a rather dark and brooding-looking automobile that had in it three rather dark and brooding-looking young men who were issuing sullen stares and obscene epithets against an unseen enemy. He watched the black car drive up and down the street and the occupants inside looking intently about, and soon it drove away; and in another minute, there came another car that was the twin of the first car, both in the animate human characters therein and the inanimate metal character without, and these young men too were uttering gross profanities and looking about with scowling countenances for some unseen nemesis; but, as it were, when this second car pulled into the parking lot of the elementary school, he felt a frosty chill seize him. He, who had been in too many places and had seen too much of this kind of hunter and hunted game, knew what was to come; and so, disobeying every lesson he had learned regarding his societal stature, he turned down the white sidewalk and quickly walked toward the school.

A lesser man would have been nervous and shaking with trepidation at the reaction he knew his appearance would elicit from parents and school officials and students, but he knew what he had to do and he was going to do it. As he walked down the path to the front office, it was as if he were a cyclone parting the sea of people before him, so swiftly did all of them flee in front of him and take refuge to his left and right and regroup behind him. He might as well have been a rabid dog come to bite everyone.

He was near the office and the adults there were already on him like a duck on a June bug, stopping his forward progress with their bodies and even threatening to physically turn him around and eject him from the premises. But it was too late. The first car full of predators had found the second car containing their prey.

He looked up and saw the first car speeding past the school and the dull, black weapons drawn and he knew what he had to do. "Get down," he shouted with all the force and fury in his soul, just as if he were yelling to his own family on that long-ago fateful day.

He knew it was too late to save everyone because of his lack of credibility as an agent of admonition to Innocents, but he did see two small children close to him and so he quickly bent down and embraced both of them.

Six shots of great magnitude exploded into the air and brought a riot of panic and desperation. Parents were screaming and teachers were shouting and students were frightened and no one could see clearly except the one man who had knelt down. The mother of these children, upon seeing this man seize them, forgot about the gunfire and the danger and moved to dislodge them from him; but when she took hold of him it was too easy, she thought, and he fell back too quickly. Soon she was hugging her precious babies, and then someone whose mind was sharper and stronger than the rest called out that someone needed to call an ambulance, and then it hit the woman directly in her throbbing brain: the man had wounds to his body, and she knew why, she knew, she just somehow knew why he had done what he had done and she suddenly felt a strange kind of guilt and grief that she had never experienced.

She knelt down next to the man and observed the enormous amount of blood upon his body, and she saw his kind face and instinctively knew that she had been wrong, terribly, terribly, and undeniably wrong about him.

"Why," she said, trembling, as she held his head in her lap and caressed his curly blond hair, "why," she whispered, for truly, she did not know.

He smiled then, a brief, gentle smile that told her he was beyond the reach of the petty world and its petty toys of violence; and as he lifted up his hands toward the still-trembling children, she brought them closer to him as he whispered in a voice that seemed to come from his immortal soul, "Greater love hath no one than this," and behold, his face became luminous, as if all that was good and loving in him now inhabited it, "that one lay down his life for his friends."

Warm and pious tears were streaming down her cheeks when she took his hands and kissed them and then held them against her face, her eyes now closed as she lovingly whispered to him, "Friend."

And then she opened her eyes, her countenance full of hope and glory as she declared, "Children, behold, Man."

And then Joe died, yet he lived—because of whom he believed in, which was evidenced by sacrificing a little bit of his life every day for the benefit of those in need around him—by gaining Paradise forever.

-Finis-